I0518286

MULBERRY TO ROME

By

Giovanni Gambino & Lance Lane

Club Lighthouse Publishing E-Book
ISBN: 978-1-927337-39-4
All rights reserved

For information contact:
comments@clublighthousepublishing.com

A Club Lighthouse Crime Drama Edition
Published in Canada

PROLOGUE

"**A**RE YOU FUCKING KIDDING me?" Tony gives Joey the direst look. Joey, average looking dark hair man in his mid thirties who is always scheming to make a few extra bucks, is sitting there with a dumbstruck look and Ralphie, not the brightest out of the bunch, is also very shocked. All three can't believe what they have just witnessed, and from the look on their faces, this is the worst thing in the world that could have happened.

"Joey, I could fucking kill you right now." All three of them just sit there staring at the TV as they show the replay. Tony, who is sick, and can't look at it again, "not once but they have to torture me with the fucking replay?" The commentator is going over the play as the TV is showing the football sailing beautifully through the goalpost. The crowd in the bar explodes each time they show it. Everyone is celebrating except for Tony, Joey and Ralphie.

Tony is still pissed off and shaking his head. He is a tall good-looking man in his mid thirties, very well dressed. He is the smartest one of the three but right now, he feels like a dumb ass for listening to Joey and his stupid predications.

They walk out of the bar and the streets are crowded with people. The Feast of San Gennaro is going on. Joey can't help but stop and smell the sizzling sausages. Tony smacks him in the head, "Move it or I will make you into a sausage." The crowd is loud and everyone is having a good time.

There is a stage set up in the middle of the block. Pretty girls and tough guys are standing around watching waiting for the next wanna be star to come up and perform. *T-Bone*, a hip-hop rapper, who is a legend in his own mind, tries to work the crowd tirelessly. The crowd just doesn't quite get him but that doesn't stop T-Bone, he is determined and is pushing onto the stage even though he senses it could get ugly. Tony cuts through the crowd and past the performing T-Bone with Joey and Ralphie on his tail like puppies. Ralphie and Joey stop for a second, look at T-Bone, then race by up to Tony. Joey turns to Tony,

"So what are we going to do?"

Tony just keeps walking, "I'm not talking to you, Joey."

"You're not talking to me, what the hell are you talking about?" Ralphie is behind Joey.

"He's not talking to you Joey."

"I heard what Tony said Ralphie, why the hell aren't you talking to me?"

Tony just keeps walking. "If I told ya, then I'd be talking to ya."

Ralphie cannot help but let out a chuckle, "that makes sense."

"How would you know if that makes sense, Ralphie you're retarded?"

Tony stops dead in his tracks. Joey and Ralphie slam on the brakes. Ralphie was still upset about what Joey has said.

"Hey, you ain't supposed to use that word."

Tony looks at Joey, "The only retard here is you Joey."

"Guys, that word retard," Ralphie is getting really pissed off.

"How am I a retard Tony?"

"Guys, really, times have changed"

"Joey you wanna know how you are a retard, *The Giants*."

"What?"

"Only a retard—"

"Whoa! The word retard, come on already you know I hate that word."

"Would bet against *The Giants*, only a severe retard would bet fifty thousand dollars." Tony starts picking up steam. "Only a stoned out of his mind retard would get his best friend, who by the way is marrying his sister, involved in another one of his retarded schemes." Ralphie has had enough.

"Okay, if I hear that word one more time, I'm going to have to put my foot in someone's ass."

Tony looks at Joey. "I thought I told you. No more schemes, no more short cuts, no more!"

"But I thought it was a sure thing. I had inside info. *The Giants* were supposed to win."

"Fuck Joey it's always a sure thing with you! You always have it in the bag and at the end we all get screwed, AND by thirty?   What the fuck were you thinking Joey?"

"Yea, by thirty, Ralphie was there he heard it too." Tony looks at Ralphie.

"Yeah, the other fucking retard."

"OH! I heard it with my own ears."

"No, no, no! Not only did they not win by thirty, they lost by a field goal, a freaking goal, three points, and now we are in the hole for fifty, fifty thousand dollars. Life is not supposed to be like this, life is supposed to be—" Suddenly something catches Tony's eye, "Shit!"

On the far street corner, a rough, tough looking guy in a jogging suit appears with a scowl. Joey and Ralphie now see the man who is coming towards them.

Joey looks at Tony, "He doesn't look so friendly."

Tony gives Joey the direst look, "Oh, you think so?" Tony, Joey and Ralphie hang a quick right on Hester. Flying around the corner, Tony and the guys stop dead in their tracks, with a look of horror on their faces. They realize the rough looking guy is racing towards them but this time he's with two rougher looking goons who are also in track suits. By the looks on their faces, they have some serious intentions. Ralphie looks at Tony with a scared but sarcastic look on his face.

"Maybe they just want to talk."

"What a—?" and before Tony could finish the sentence Joey does it for him.

"RETARD"

"Hey!"

Tony and Joey grab Ralphie and race back down Mott Street towards Canal Street. They cause traffic by running across the street, car horns are blaring and tires screeching. The rough looking guy and the two goons are right on their tail as they run across the busy street. Tony and the boys run into a Chinese curio shop, they try to disguise themselves with straw hats and Chinese robes. The three goons look around and spot their targets. Tony realizes they are caught, and they dash through the crowd in the shop and head out the back door. As they are running, Tony is cursing, and vows never to listen to this son of bitch ever again. Poor Joey can't help but think this is his fault.

Tony screams at him, "It is your fault, you fucking idiot! If I would've minded my business I wouldn't be doing this work out right now."

Ralphie, trying to get his mind off the goons, says to Tony, "Cardio is the best work out." Tony shakes his head; "how did I get stuck with these fucking retards?" Racing down the cobblestone alley, Tony and the guys strip off their robes and hats and run for their lives. As the cars and truck horns blast once again, Tony, Joey and Ralphie, race across Canal Street and up Elizabeth Street. Flying up the street, Tony, Joey and Ralphie, are almost home, when out of a doorway steps out Sal. Sal is a tall big guy in his forties. He's a rough looking character and always wears a suit. Sal was blocking the doorway, eating an apple, just waiting for the boys to show up. He smiles when he sees Tony and the guys, who stop dead in their tracks. They finally realized the race was over.

Sal smirks, "Tony, Joey and Ralphie just the guys we wanted to see."

Tony looks around and sees the guy with the two goons who have their bats ready. He looks back at Sal who takes a deep breath and wags a finger at all three of them.

"Hey, you guys weren't going to leave were you?"

Tony takes a deep breath as Joey and Ralphie try to catch their breath from all the running. "No Sal, we would never." Tony looks at his boys and they turn around and run across the street sideways, bursting through the doors of a pet store. The store is full of barking dogs, meowing cats, and for some reason, at least six miniature horses.

Joey stops and looks at Ralphie, "what the fuck is that?"

They continue to run when a screaming woman tries to stop them but Tony and the guys keep hauling, heading to the back door as the birds fly out.

On the stage, T-Bone is now in a fight for his life! As he tries to rap, shoes, food, and anything that can be thrown, is flying at him. He keeps ducking and rapping, knowing no matter what the show must go on. Tony, Joey and Ralphie, dash through near riotous crowd and by *T-Bone* heading for the doorway of an Old Italian Coffee Shop across the street. Sal and the boys are still on their trail as they come out flying out of the pet store with feathers flying all over them. Tony sees them coming and continues to run into the coffee shop when suddenly they stop dead in their tracks. The coffee shop is your typical Italian set up. You have your gangsters drinking their espresso and playing cards. The older ones where telling wild stories to the young and new gangsters. It has black tinted windows so you couldn't see in. The bartender is cleaning the glasses as Tony and the boys walk in. They all stop and look at the boys. Tony not knowing what to say finally speaks.

"This isn't Starbucks is it?"

Sal and his crew are standing behind Tony and the guys;

"No, No it's not. Don Luciano wants to see you."

CHAPTER ONE
An Offer The Boys Can't Refuse

SAL LEADS TONY AND the panicked Joey and Ralphie towards the back of the shop. Behind the desk sits Don Luciano, a man in his sixties, heavy set in a silk smoking jacking. He stands up, holding his cat, as he sees the boys coming in. As Don Luciano pets the cat, Sal is breathing, standing behind Tony, breathing down his neck. Don Luciano gives Sal a look to step back. "You have to excuse the mess."

Tony and the guys look over and see some workmen rolling up a rug. Joey gives Tony a really nervous look and Don Luciano sees this. "There was a stain."

Tony then notices a pair of feet in nice Italian leather loafers sticking out of the rolled-up rug, Tony nudges Joey who sees, and starts to freak. Don Luciano turns, still petting the cat that is purring and looks at Tony and the guys, with steely eyes. "Some people are dog people but me I'm a cat person. You wanna know why?"

Tony clears his throat, "Their independence?"

Don Luciano smiles, "they hate rats." Don Luciano looks at the rolled up rug, "and so do I." He puts the cat down and smiles at the boys. "I have a question for you boys." As the workmen carry out the rug that obviously has a body in it, Joey can't take it any longer. "Look Don Luciano, sir, your honour, now I think I have an answer to all of your problems." Tony can't believe what he just heard and gives Joey a, *'I'm going to fuck you up'* look,

"You do?"

Ralphie also in shock, then again, when isn't Ralphie confused? "You do?"

Joey smiles, "I sure do. This morning I got a hell of a tip. Not like last time, I'm telling you this time, a home run. All I need is fifty thousand."

Tony can't stop from speaking up, "Don Luciano, please don't listen to him, he's crazy." Joey smiles with his wicked '*I'm really fucked up*' smile, "crazy like a fox."

Ralphie, being the slow one out of the bunch, looks really confused., "Like a fox? How the hell is a fox—" before he can finish the sentence, he gets a smack on the back of his head from Sal,

"Give it a rest, numb nuts, let the boss hear Joey's idea."

Joey smiles, "Thank you Sal. Now the way I got it figured, we owe you fifty so give us another fifty. I know what you're thinking but this information I have is good. I take the odds place the bet and BINGO, BANGO, BONGO, give you back the hundred thousand plus the vig and we are all friends once again."

Tony just looks down and shakes his head. At this point he is sick to his stomach with all of Joey's stupid schemes.

Sal can't help but look confused, "Bingo, Bango, Bongo? That's not even Italian, what the hell is wrong with you? I ought to shoot you just for saying that. "Sal reaches for his gun but Tony jumps in to help his friend Joey.

"You have to forgive the idiot Don Luciano; on the way here today he slipped and hit his head. He doesn't know what he is saying." Tony swallows really hard and gets serious. "Don Luciano as you know, I have always been loyal and shown respect in both my actions and deeds. And I have always thought of you as a father, and I hope to one day be treated as one of your sons. Now I should have been more careful in my associations and having made a terrible mistake." Tony shoots Joey a look. "I will not stop working until the debt."

Don Luciano smiles and puts up his hand silencing Tony.

"I'll try this again you boys don't seem to listen. Can I ask you boys a question?"

The boys all look at each other and nod,

"Sure, yea, of course."

With a smile and evil look, Don Luciano looks at them, "Do you boys like to fish?"

In confusion, Tony, Joey and Ralphie, look at each other not knowing what to say...

* * * * *

ALL THREE BOYS ON sitting on the deck of a huge yacht blindfolded with gags in their mouth. Don Luciano and his boys stand around them. "Oh what a beautiful day, the sun is shining the birds are singing and the waves are nice and big, what do you think boys?" Sal took the gag out of Tony's mouth. Tony is scared shitless of what is going to happen, knowing that bad intentions fill the air,

"Ah Don Luciano honestly, I can't see shit with this blindfold and I'm getting a little sea sick." Sal sticks the gag back in his mouth, "oh shut up you stupid prick." Don Luciano continues to teach the boys a lesson.

"Now you are going to learn what happens to those who try and steal from me."

Tony and guys, even though gagged, muffle strong protest. Don Luciano smirks

"No, no that's what you were trying to do, steal and this is what I do to thieves; throw the bastards overboard!"

Don Luciano motions to Sal, who with some of the others, grab Tony, Joey and Ralphie who scream muffled screams. The boys go flying over the yachts railing towards the water. They hit the water and go under. They pop up and the blindfolds come off and they are standing in water only up to their chest. Don Luciano, Sal and the others still on the boat laughing and smoking cigars.

"You got lucky it's low tide, next time you won't be so lucky it will be high tide. You got till Saturday or you're dead!"

Tony, Joey and Ralphie, soaked, nod, not wanting to die.

CHAPTER TWO
Choose Your Friends

SOAKED TO THE BONE, the boys walk up the street towards Rosalina Rosa's "Super Psychic" storefront. Tony stops and stares at the both of them

"Okay that's it! I don't ever want to see you two again!"

"But you are marrying my sister."

"That reminds me, you come to the wedding I will personally put a bullet in you."

Ralphie trying to make a case for him looks at Tony,

"Why me, I've known you since we were kids and we went to P.S.128 together."

Tony stops, takes a breath, and stops. "Okay, I'll see you Ralphie, but Joey, no way."

Joey can't believe it, "What? That's not fair; you're banging my sister. That has to count for something?"

"Yeah I pray our kids don't come out with your genes!"

Suddenly, Rosalina Rosa, a very hot looking gypsy babe in her twenties, pops out of the doorway of her psychic shop and is face to face with Tony.

"Your aura is speaking to me, you are in danger." Ralphie stops and looks at her.

"You think so?"

"I am Rosalina Rosa, super psychic." Tony looks at her.

13

"Thanks but no thanks."

"Please you must come with me." She grabs his hand and starts to pull Tony towards her shop.

"Hey I don't—"

"You must come with me." Tony pulls his arm away and steps back. Ralphie looks at Tony

"Tony, I think she needs to talk."

"I knew your name was Tony." Joey looks at her in shock

"Whoa she's good!"

"She just heard you say my name asshole."

"Tony we must talk, you need to hear what I have to say."

"Get out of here! You're as crazy as these two idiots, as a matter of fact why don't you take them and talk to them?" Tony starts to walk and Rosalina races up to hand Tony her card. "Here's my card please call me." Pocketing the card, Tony keeps walking as Joey and Ralphie catch up, leaving Rosalina behind.

"She knew we were in trouble."

"It's a scam Ralphie."

"How could it be a scam, she knew."

"Cause fifty percent of everyone in this neighbourhood is in trouble, it's pretty simple odds."

Joey sees his chance as the three continue to walk.

"That's right fifty percent just like the trouble we are in. It's not really that big of a deal, right Tony?" Tony continues to ignore him and doesn't answer him.

"Tony come on, I screwed up but got to talk to me." Tony stops and just looks at Joey.

"Screwed up, this is more than a screw up. I'm getting married to your sister next week." He looks around to make sure the coast is clear. All he sees is a Lucy's Sausage Truck with a huge rubber sausage stuck on top turn the corner. "I was supposed to have my *Omertá* at the end of the week, now it looks like I'll be having my last rites.

Joey rolls his eyes, "you worry too much."

"Me worry, are you really fucked up in the head? I've worked very hard at my profession. The honour of being "made" is only offered to a selected few. I have proven with my loyalty, hard work, and discipline, that I, Tony Magliocco, am one of those few.

Joey looks at Ralphie, "see this is why my sister is such a lucky woman." Tony just shakes his head,

"Stop kissing my ass you brown nose fuck, how can you let this happen? You told me you had a fool proof tip."

"We did, we heard it from the owner of the team."

"What?"

"Yeah the owner, tell him Ralphie."

"Yeah we were over at the Vegas Diner in Bensonhurst and the owner was talking about the game."

Ralphie and Joey think back on the day that they heard about the big tip. They were sitting at the booth next to a heavy set man in his sixties who was dressed from head to toe in *New York Giants* gear and were talking adamantly on his cell phone. The diner was very

crowded. A huge banner out front of the diner, read...
Welcome Brooklyn's NFL Football Fantasy League.

"Tony you don't understand, he was talking about trading players and cutting deals."

Ralphie looks at Tony trying to defend Joey, "You could tell he was someone!"

"What the hell was the owner of the *New York Giants* doing at the Vegas Diner you fucking idiots, it was a freaking Fantasy Football League convention! What the fuck did you think, that he heard about their famous strawberry cheesecake and he just had to go have a piece? YOU ARE RETARDS one more stupid than the other!"

Tony is now pissed off and seeing red as Joey and Ralphie are trying to calm him down.

"Your sister is going to kill me! All she talks about is when I go to work for Don Luciano." From the corner of his eye Tony sees Lucy's Sausage Truck turn the corner. He doesn't pay any attention to it and continues to talk to his boys. "She's been telling all her friends, spending money on the wedding. If Don Luciano doesn't kill me she will. I am a dead man and I have my future fucking brother in law to thank for it because he happened to hear a man talking about the *Giants!*"

"We'll figure something out." Ralphie looks at Joey

"Yeah we got the smarts to figure something out."

Both Tony and Joey look at Ralphie and roll their eyes. Ralphie gets all insecure,

"What?" Tony snaps at him and takes a deep breathe

"Smarts? You and smart in the same sentence? Are you fucking kidding me? I AM A DEAD MAN! Life is

not supposed to be like this, life is supposed to be—"
Suddenly something catches Tony's eye. "Shit."

A small little dog wearing a *Giants* jersey darts out of
a doorway and runs up the block right into the path of
Lucy's Sausage Truck.   A little old lady in a bath robe
screams as she sees the small little dog about to get run
over by the truck.   The driver in the truck honks and
blasts his horn and veers off the road. He ends up on the
sidewalk to miss the dog.   With the look of horror on
their faces, it drives straight at Tony, Joey and Ralphie.
At the last possible moment, all three dive out of the way
as the out of control Sausage Truck just misses them as it
roars by.   Joey and Ralphie collect themselves, Tony
watches as the Sausage Truck regains control. Tony then
locks eyes with Rosalina, who is just staring at him from
her doorway. Tony jumps up, and grabs the others.

"Let's get the hell out of here!"

Rosalina smiles and with her finger motions for Tony
to join her.   Ralphie was still in shock, "that bastard
almost killed us!" Tony is freaked out about the whole
situation, not only did Rosalina tell him that he was in
danger but he was just about to get hit by a truck because
a little dog with *GIANTS* shirt ran in his path.

"What are the fucking odds? Let's get the hell out of
here."

Joey looks and sees Rosalina; "hey the fortune teller
was right, and you were almost." Tony realizing what
Joey was about to say, "Let's GO NOW!" Tony takes off
and Joey and Ralphie follow as Rosalina watches.

CHAPTER THREE
F.E.A.R – False, Evidence That Appears Real

TONY LIVES WITH HIS fiancée, Donna in Bensonhurst, in a nice cozy brownstone. Donna is in her late twenties, very beautiful, tall and skinny with long light brown hair, and very materialistic. She likes money and knows how to spend it. Tony knows that once she finds out what just went down she is going to flip out! Tony, Joey, and Ralphie, stand outside the brownstone, practicing what he is going to say. Tony almost has his speech down.

"Donna my love I know you were looking forward to me working in Don Luciano's company and the wealth and respect it would bring BUT..."

Joey and Ralphie knowing how Donna can get, sneak away as Tony is practicing. Tony has no clue that the boys just ditched him! He continues thinking the boys are right there by his side.

"Donna our love is more important than money, and respect we can be happy even if I drive a cab." He smiles at what he came up with, he turns around to tell the boys, "Hey guys I think I got it, Donna will—" And that's when he realizes they are gone. They have left him. He has to face his bridezilla alone.

Looking up and down the block, Tony takes a deep breath, walks up the steps and goes into the brownstone. After a moment, the afternoon silence is shattered. Donna Sanzone is pissed! Tony tries to tell her the events of the day and she's on the verge of losing it big time!

"WHAT THE FUCK?!! This cannot be happening. Let me get this straight, you owe Don Luciano fifty thousand dollars and if you don't pay him, you won't work for him?"

"If I don't pay him he will kill me."

"So you will not work for him?"

"Babe I won't be working for anyone if I'm dead!"

"How the hell did this happen?" Tony, facing the fire, takes a breath.

"Your brother"

"My brother Joey? I told you not to hang out with that fucking idiot!"

"But he's your brother."

"So I should know him more than anyone, he and Ralphie are the biggest losers in all of Brooklyn!"

Tony knows this was going to happen, he knows she would flip out. He has had a long day and decides he is going to sit down to take a load off.

"Oh no you don't, you are not sitting down. You are going to take care of this."

"But how do I?"

"That's not my problem it's yours!" Donna gets in Tony's face, "I've waited too long for this." Tears start to form in her eyes, "If I have to hear Connie Cangelosi brag about all the respect her husband has one more day, I'm going to put a bullet in my head!" Donna looks at Tony in the eyes. "Better yet maybe I will put a bullet in your head."

Tony shakes his head in disbelief and wonders to himself *why am I marrying this woman? Oh yeah she's fucking hot!*

"You don't mean that, plus I'll be dead already if I don't pay back the money!"

Donna steps closer to Tony, so close that her nose is touching his, "Tony you know me and you know what happens if you disappoint me?" She puts her arms around him, "now I want you to take care of this, promise?" Tony can't resist Donna, she is an amazing lover and he knows that if he loses her his sex life will never be the same. Just the thought of it was getting him all hot and bothered. Tony nods his head like the puppet that he is.

"I want to hear you say promise."

"I promise."

"I don't believe you, say it again."

"I promise"

Anger flashes in Donnas' eyes, and she starts to twist Tony's arm.

"Say it again."

"I promise."

"AGAIN!"

"Hey that's starting to hurt."

"SAY IT."

"I PROMISE!"

Donna lets go of Tony's arm, "I believe you honey, now go make Donna proud."

Tony's seizes the moment and heads for the door. Donna screams out to Tony has he heads for the door.

"The wedding is Saturday I want this taken care of before that!" Tony is out the door before Donna can really get going on her rant.

*   *   *   *   *

NOT KNOWING WHAT TO do Tony starts to walk around and think. He can't take it anymore and as he is just sits sitting on a bench, all alone, Tony looks at the Manhattan skyline, knowing there is no way to raise the money. There is only one thing he can do. He understands now how people get thoughts of suicide in their heads. He heads to the Verrazano Bridge. As the cars whiz by, Tony is on the Verrazano Bridge, has thoughts no man should have. He stares at the water below and wonders how cold it could possible be, how fast will it take before his life is actually over? All these thoughts run through his head but he is unable to jump. He thinks to himself, *"Maybe I can go somewhere that's not so high."* Now a little closer to earth, Tony is on the end of a pier, and looks down, but once again, can't do it. *"Is this really worth my life? But at the end, either way I'm going to end up dead."* He decides water is not the way to go, he wants something that's going to be fast and that he won't remember the pain. Now even closer to earth, on a roof of one-story building on 3rd Avenue, Tony looks down, but once again, can't do it. "Oh fuck this I'm going to go see my *Nonna!*"

*   *   *   *   *

 T ONY HEADS OVER TO Coney Island Hospital where his *Nonna*, in her late sixties, is lying laying in her hospital bed with her eyes shut. She's hooked up to all these complicated looking machines. Tony sits next to his *Nonna* and starts to have a conversation with her while she's sleeping.

"I have failed at everything *Nonna.* My wedding to Donna, *finito!* Me becoming part of the Luciano organization, *finito!* Me every making you proud, *finito!* As a grandson I am the biggest." Tony couldn't finish, tears come to out of his eyes and suddenly *Nonna* opens her eyes and looks at Tony.

"Tony, *sangue mio*, is that you?"

"*Nonna, si* it's me."

"What the fuck! I was trying to sleep and you wake me up crying like a little fucking girl? Boo-Hoo Donna doesn't want to marry me, boo-Hoo Don Luciano doesn't like me, Boo-Hoo I'm a fucking loser!" *Nonna* sits up in bed and smacks Tony in the head, "I've got news for you Tony, you come from a long line of losers." Tony looks at his *Nonna* and is in shock, "what the hell are you talking about?" *Nonna* shakes her head as she goes back and tells Tony about his family history.

"Back in the day your *Nonno* wanted nothing but to be part of the Palmero Family. The only thing he had to do to be part of the family was shoot straight."

Little Italy 1921

Tony's Grandfather was in his early thirties, hiding behind the corner building looking at the Olive Oil

Company. A sedan pulls up and an evil looking heavyset man in his fifties dressed in a flamboyant suit gets out and heads for the Oil Company. Tony's Grandfather steps out and pulls out a gun, as he fires, the man in the suit notices his shoe is un-tied, and bends down to tie it. The bullet misses and ricochets off the metal step handrail, off the lamppost, then off the copper building rook, and right into Tony's grandfather, who falls down and dies! *Nonna* proceeds to tell Tony about his father. "All your father had to do was light a little fire and he would be a made member of the Catania Family. She brings Tony back to an old warehouse in Red Hook Brooklyn. His father, a man in his forties, a tough looking man, is all smiles as he just finished emptying the five gallon gas can on the outside of the building, but he doesn't see the trail of dangerous gasoline that leads back to him. He steps back, he lights the lighter and he tosses it towards the building. The building is in flames but then the fire starts to race right back towards Tony's father. In horror, his father starts to run but doesn't drop the can! The poor man cannot outrun the flames. *Nonna* shakes her head, "What a *fesso!*" Tony father is blown up in a huge explosion. *Nonna* looks at Tony dead in the eyes, "The curse of the Magliocco's ends today! You are going to grow some balls and get the job done and become a made man! If you don't" *Nonna* leans forward, "I will kill you myself. Now get the hell out of here, *Deal Or No Deal* is coming on." Tony leans over to his *Nonna*, kisses her, and gets the hell out of the room, nodding his head on the way out.

CHAPTER FOUR
Greatest Message Tony Ever Preached

TONY AND THE BOYS are standing at the center of the world's greatest bridge, the Brooklyn Bridge. Tony looks at Ralphie and Joey.

"You're probably wondering what the hell we're doing here?"

Joey looks around, "I'm not jumping."

Ralphie confused as always, "We're jumping?"

"No you fucking idiots, we are not jumping."

Ralphie looks at Joey, "I'm too young to die."

"We'll figure something out.   Jumping is not the answer."

Tony looks at the boys and rolls his eyes, "we're not jumping."

Ralphie still confused, "you know Tony it's an unforgivable sin that is what we are about to do."

Tony looks at both of them, "What the hell are you talking about?"

"Jumping off this bridge."

Tony sees red, he's so pissed.

"We're not jumping?" Ralphie looks around and still no answer from Tony. "Then what the fuck are we doing on a bridge?"

Joey looks at Ralphie, "Makes sense to me, bridges are made to jump off.'

Tony is now officially pissed off and had enough of these two fucking idiots and flips out on the both of them. "No! No! We are not jumping off the bridge but I may throw you off if you don't shut the fuck up but the rest of us ain't jumping."

Joey and Ralphie look at Tony,

"So you brought us up here to kill us?"

"No, no! No one is going to die. I brought you there to the Brooklyn Bridge cause this is the greatest thing an Italian has ever done, built this bridge! And if an Italian can do this we can get Don Luciano his money. I can be made and Donna can have her wedding!"

Ralphie takes a breath and Joey is the confused one now. "Ah, Tony the guy that made this bridge was named Roebling, he was German." Ralphie all interested in the new information he learned.

"Really a German, no way!"

"Yeah it says so on the sign." Ralphie points to the sign. Tony and Joey look at the sign, Tony looks around, "Okay, a German Huh? Well if he did this even though he wasn't Italian we can do it, if each of us tries to get the money by Saturday, this little problem of ours will be history." Tony throws his arms around the guys and starts to walk.

A calendar page that reads Saturday floats in air over the scowling face of Donna, then over the evil grinning face of Sal...Meanwhile at COLUMBO'S CLAM HOUSE, LITTLE ITALY, The famous old joint sits in the afternoon sun. Tony walks in and heads straight to the back booth where he sees his Uncle Al sitting there with a quizzical look on his face. Uncle Al is an overweight older man in his sixties. Tony sits down and tries to explain to his Uncle his situation and if he can help by lending him some money. Uncle Al looks at Tony, very confused, and tries to make sense of the conversation.

"I don't know what the hell you're talking about. I got... I got... What the hell is the name of the disease where you forget everything?" Tony looks at him,

"Alzheimer?"

"See, I forgot."

"Stop it! You don't have Alzheimer, Uncle Al. Listen, I just need to borrow fifty- thousand" Al looks at Tony tries to play it off as if he's confused.

"Uncle Al, I don't know anyone named Uncle Al, and I don't know you. So, sorry but I can't give you any money."

"I have to have the money by next week, you don't understand." Uncle Al is distracted by the hot little waitress he smiles and quickly says to her,

"Honey, remember I like pasta Al Dente." The waitress stops and smiles.

"I know, I know, I've been coming here for forty-five years, but a man's pasta, should be a little stiff." Al winks at the waitress, and then mouths "Call Me later". Uncle Al realizes that he's being watched by Tony. "Oh, wait a minute, do I like pasta? Where am I? Alzheimer, it's such a cruel disease." Tony glares at his uncle.

"You don't want to lend me the money, do you Uncle Al?"

"Uncle Al, I'm related to you?" Tony just shakes his head, he gets up, says goodbye to his Uuncle, and leaves.

Calendar page that reads Sunday floats in the air over the scowling face of Donna, then over the evil grinning face of Sal.

As the days pass, Tony has to figure out what to do for money. He decides that he's going to Sid's Pawn shop to sell his beloved bust of Frank Sinatra. In the meantime Joey and Ralphie are stealing lemonade money from a bunch of crying kids. Ralphie can't help but think how bad that is. "Joey we need to go to church, this is bad, maybe we will get some kind of inspiration there."

Joey looks at Ralphie, thinking what a fucking retard, but then gets a really wicked idea. "Ok that sounds like a good idea." So they go the old Gothic Church that overlooks Bensonhurst. Joey and Ralphie are sitting in the back of the pew in the crowded church and Joey puts a big smile on his face. Ralphie, at first, is confused and starts to look around, then he realizes the reason and starts to smile too. The parishioners were passing money, lots of money to the waiting ushers with baskets, as the priest looks on. Joey gets an idea and whispers in Ralphie's ear.

Ralphie smiles, "I told you we would get an inspiration if we came to church." They both get up and leave.

That night Joey and Ralphie head back to the church. They clumsily slip through a window into the empty church. They go towards the huge altar and suddenly Ralphie stops and looks at the statue of Jesus Christ on the cross. Joey continues on and then notices that Ralphie is no longer with him and goes back to get him. Ralphie was feeling a little guilty about stealing from the church. He looks at Joey. "I got a bad feeling about this."

Joey is trying to justify what they are doing, looks at the statue of Jesus Christ on the cross.

"Okay, Lord if you don't want us to take the money, nod your head." They look at the statue and nothing happens. "Looks like the money is ours." Joey and Ralphie once again head for the altar, then cut to the left and disappear behind the thick red curtains. All you hear is banging and smashing and you see Joey and Ralphie come running out, carrying a huge tithing box full of cash. They race out the side door to the alley. As they are running down the alley, someone jumps right in front of them. It's a Ninja Priest, standing in a fighting pose. They stop dead in their tracks, then turn and start to run with the tithing box back towards the church. Another Ninja Priest lands and strikes a fighting pose ready to kick ass. Knowing an ass kicking is coming, looks of horror come to Joey's and Ralphie's faces. Ralphie can't help but tell Joey, "I told you this wasn't a good idea." Joey just looks at Ralphie and hisses, "Shut the fuck up!"

CHAPTER FIVE
The Art Of Self-Motivation

A CALENDAR PAGE THAT reads Thursday floats in air the over the scowling face of Donna, than over the evil grinning face of Sal.

Outside of the world famous diner, Tony, Joey and Ralphie, who look the worst from the beating they took from the Ninja priests, lean on the hood of Joey's Chevy, eating a piece of probably the best cheesecake in the world. "It was wrong trying to rob the church. You don't fuck with God, nothing good ever comes out of that. You see what you got for it, two fucking idiots trying to rob a church!" Tony looks at the two and continues "I didn't know Father Roy was such a tough?"

Joey holds up his hand to shut Tony up, "Please, I just want to eat my cheesecake." Tony still trying to figure a way to get the money, looks at Joey, "we just need a break, something to just go our way." Suddenly a black Cadillac comes roaring up and screeches to a stop. Out jumps a very angry Donna and sees her man eating Cheesecake.

"Cheesecake, Cheesecake? You got two days you stupid bastard! Two days! Two days until I am a lovely bride!" She shoots a look at Joey and Ralphie and rolls her eyes. She points at all three of them. "You guys screw this up, and God as my witness, I'll kill all three of you!" She gets back in her car and tires smoke as the car races off. Ralphie looks at Tony, "You are one lucky man Tony."

Poor Tony has had enough and just shakes his head, "life is not supposed to be like this." As he reaches in his pocket, he pulls out the card Rosalina Rosa, the psychic, gave him. "Life is supposed to be." Tony looks at the back of card, "Oh what the fuck is this?" On the back of the card are is the numbers 2, 3, 33, 10, 5 are written. "I guess these are supposed to be my lucky numbers." Tony looks up and sees a big clock across the street, it reads two o'clock. Then a set of identical triplets comes walking across the street at him. Not believing what he is seeing, a truck dries by with a billboard ad, reading, 33 Exciting Flavours of Ice Tea! "What the hell... Thirty three?" Tony looks at the card in awe, as Joey and Ralphie look at him like he is crazy.

Tony looks up and sees ten school children, in matching uniforms, walking down the street, in a row, holding hands. "No way, ten kids." He looks and sees five nuns in habits drive by in a convertible Mustang. "Five nuns! My god, these are my lucky numbers! That crazy psychic chick was right! She wanted to give me these numbers. We have to play the lotto!" Ralphie looks at the card, while something across the street has gotten all of Joey's attention. "When you win the prize money, get a lump sum. They'll tax the hell out of you if you take yearly payments." Tony just rolls his eyes at Ralphie, "I knew somehow it would work." Tony runs across the street to the bodega. The boys look after him. He comes running out, waving a lotto ticket. Tony screams from across the street, "This is the answer to all our problems. We're going to win, I can feel it." Joey nodded his head, "Put away the lotto ticket, I got the real answer to all our problems. Joey is still looking across the street. A skinny mousey man named Jimmy two-shoes is hurriedly walking down the street. Tony looks at Joey, "you think I'm going to listen to you? We are in this fucking mess because of you! Plus all the numbers matched, it's a sign to play the lotto." Joey points to a billboard advertising the Lotto for the following week. "The lotto is Tuesday, three days after the wedding but there's your sign." Joey points to Jimmy Two-Shoes, now excitedly talking to another man across the street. "There's the answer." Tony can't even begin to understand Joey anymore, "Jimmy Two-Shoes?' Joey smiles, 'That's right, Jimmy two-Shoes, by Saturday my friend, you will be married, a made man, and we will all be rich!" Jimmy Two-Shoes starts to walk off and Tony and the boys follow. Jimmy Two-Shoes goes in and quickly backs out of a seedy bar as Tony, Joey and Ralphie watch in Joey's Chevy. Jimmy is talking to a man outside of a bodega, then he is off again;, Tony and the boys follow in the car. Coming out of a strip bar, Jimmy heads down the street. Tony and Ralphie are watching as Joey comes out of a toy store and joins them with a bag under his arm. He jumps into the car and they continue following Jimmy Two-Shoes.

CHAPTER SIX

The Fellas You Keep Will Have
A Positive Or Negative Impact

IT WAS LATER THAT night at Rosalina Rosa "Super Psychic" Shop. Amongst all the "mysterious" and "supernatural" trappings, sits Rosalina, looking into a crystal ball. There's a knock at the door, and Rosalina looks up. She stands and walks to the door, opens it, and comes face to face with T-Bone.

"I don't think you know what the hell you're talking about lady."

Rosalina just looks at him confused. "The only thing I am going to be famous for is being the rapper that got killed by a—" T-Bone holds up a woman's shoe, "a seven and half pump! You don't know the future. I want my money back." As Rosalina stands there, she sees the old Chevy across the street. In the car Tony, Joey and Ralphie are waiting. As Rosalina stares at the car she says to T-Bone, "don't worry, you will be famous, come in, I will read your cards." Rosalina shuts the door.

Joey is behind the wheel and Tony is sitting in the front and Ralphie in the backseat. Suddenly Joey sees Lucy's Sausage Truck drive by and sees Jimmy two-shoes standing there in front of the Old Coney Island Carousel house. Tony is still confused and asks Joey, "I want to know," and just before he can finish his question, a Lincoln pulls up, and out comes out Sal and guys. They all head into the Old Carousel house and Joey starts to tap on the steering wheel with his hand, "I wonder what the hell Sal is doing there?" Tony has finally lost all his patience with Joey, his face is beat red from the blood boiling to his head, "More importantly Joey, I'll say it one more time, what the fuck are we doing here?"

In the backseat Ralphie pulls a plastic Al Pacino mask out of the bag, "and why the hell do we have Al Pacino masks and guns?" Joey smiles, "don't worry, the guns are not real and they shoot blanks." Joey takes a deep breath and shakes his head, "listen boys, genius is about to happen. That's Don Luciano's numbers bank right across the street. There has to be at least two maybe three-hundred thousand dollars cash in there."

Tony starts to go into shock; he is going to fuck Joey up with all his stupid schemes. "Have you lost your mind?"

"Brilliance my friend, now we hit it and we get the fifty we owe Don Luciano, a little on the side for us, and then—"

"We end up dead you stupid fuck!" Tony responds.

"No, no, no." Joey grabs the mask out of Ralphie's hand and looks at Tony. "Then you show up with the Al Pacino masks, you tell Sal and his goons that you tracked down the robbers, killed them and as proof, you have the masks. You give back the rest of the money except for the little we took on the side, and everyone is happy."

Ralphie, being in his own world as usual, looks at the masks, "is this Pacino from Scarface?" Joey just rolls his eyes and nods. Ralphie, is like a kid in a candy store, and grabs the mask, "it's mine."

Joey barks right back at him, "I wanted that one, you can get the Corleone Pacino mask."

As they are both fighting about the mask, Tony starts to freak out., "STOP IT! STOP IT! This is insane. We can't rob Don Luciano's numbers bank wearing Al Pacino mask and using fake guns, there's got to be a better way of getting the money." Joey and Ralphie look at Tony for an answer and with no response. Joey fires up the Chevy. Tony looks at Joey screams in horror! "No freaking way!" Joey smiles and revs the engine.

* * * * *

INSIDE AN OLD CONEY Island Carousel House at night the ugly face of Matty "Bull Dog" Amatto, *il capo* in the Castelletti family, is making arrangements. "And you are going to whack Don Luciano?" Sal and Bull Dog are standing face to face with Jimmy Two-Shoes, with Sal's guys standing across from Bull Dog's guys.

"That's why I called this little meeting. I whack Don Luciano, you whack Don Amatto, and we are the new bosses and we all become rich!" Bull Dog is not quite sold on the idea.

"How do I know I can trust you…can I trust you?" Both men just stare at each other.

"You can't."

"Neither can you." Bull Dog smiles, "I like an honest man. Looks like we are going to be the new bosses!" All of Bull Dog's men nod and smile as does Jimmy Two-Shoes and Sal's Guys. Wood flies as Joey's Chevy smashes through the door. Wearing the Al Pacino masks, Tony, Joey, and Ralphie, come out of the car with the fake guns! Tony screams. "Put your hands up!" Sal, Bull Dog, and the others, startled, start to reach for their guns. Tony fires off a wicked round of blanks from the machine gun! Not knowing they're blanks, Sal, Bull Dog, Jimmy Two-Shoes, and others, throw up their hands.

Joey is right behind Tony. "That's more like it!" Tony, still in the lead, barks out some orders, "if anybody does anything stupid, they're going to get hurt! We are here for Don Luciano's bank."

Sal looks at Tony, Joey, and Ralphie, in their Al Pacino masks. "What the hell? Al Pacino masks?" Joey insisting on the Tony's orders, "Don Luciano's numbers bank, we want it!" Sal looks at the boys, "do you know who we are?"

Tony is losing his patience, "I warned you about being stupid." He shoots another round of blanks to scare the boys. Sal, Bull Dog, and the others, jump back, putting their hands even higher. Tony gets louder after the last round of shots, "WE WANT THE BANK!"

Sal is not appreciating being yelled at. "There ain't no bank here, we were just getting ready to play cards that's all."

Joey looks around and is very confused, "we don't believe you Sal." Sal smiles, realizing who they are. Bull Dog is confused on how the masked man knows his name,

"How do punks like you know his name?"

"Yea, retards like you guys-"

Ralphie, of course, sees red. "Retards, well only a RETARD, and I will let you know that word is not to be used, would hang with Matty "'Bull Dog'" Amatto, *capo* of the Castelletti family."

"So you know who I am?" Ralphie shakes his head. "Yea duh, hey Joey I wonder what Don Luciano would say if he found out who Sal was hanging out with."

Joey couldn't believe that Ralphie just called his name, don't call me Joey, Ralphie. Sal is now convinced who the fucking retards really are, "Joey, Ralphie?"

Joey quickly looks at Tony. "Oh shit Tony, he knows who we are."

Tony can't believe what just went down he fires off a round and starts to yell louder than before. "Everyone shut the fuck up! We're here for the money!"

Sal listens, than gets very serious, "could you speak again, I think I heard that voice before." Tony doesn't say anything. "Come on say something." Not a peep from Tony. "Come on, say something," finally Tony breaks and tries to conceal his voice. "No." Sal had a smile from ear to ear,

"Tony Magliocco, that's you right?"

"No."

"It is."

"No!" Tony said it even quicker than before so that Sal couldn't pick up the voice but he knew the two fucking retards gave it away. He thought for a second and wondered why he listened to that prick Joey again! Sal shakes his head. "Well that's too bad Tony. Word can't be getting out about me and Bull Dog meeting like this. Some people might be thinking that we have plans on taking over." Tony, Joey and Ralphie, shake their heads.

"It never crossed our minds." Tony looks at Joey to shut up. "We are not saying we are Joey, Tony and Ralphie, just wanted to rob Don Luciano's bank and since it's not here" Ralphie begins to worry and finishes Tony's sentence, "We should go."

Sal gets deadly serious. "See if, someone thought that, we'd have to kill 'em."

Joey does the only thing he can. "Oh yeah, well not if we kill you first!"

Tony looks at Joey like he is crazy. "What the hell are you?" Joey fires a burst right at Sal and Bull Dog and the others dive for cover. Hitting the floor Sal, Bull Dog, and others, quickly realize that Tony is shooting blanks, when none of them are hit! "Blanks, kill them!" Tony, Joey and Ralphie, race for the door as Sal, Bull Dog, and the others, pull their guns and fire! As a hail of bullets fly around them, Tony, Joey and Ralphie, cross the street and into the bizarrely painted Coney Island Circus Sideshow. An extremely tattooed Barker around his twenties, greets Tony and boys, as they run across the street. "Come on in." Rounds start to smash all around! The Barker looks and sees Sal, Bull Dog and the others shooting! "What the hell?" The scared Barker dives for cover as Tony and Joey race into the building. The boys are running through the eccentric lobby of the sideshow, they race for the stairs. Tony, Joey and Ralphie, race by Serpentine, the snake woman, as shots ring out with Sal, Bull Dog, and the others, on their tail. Tony and the boys run by the electrifying twisted Shock Meister, then fly past Bambi, The Mermaid, who dives for cover. Sal and the others run by firing hot rounds of lead and racing up the stairs.

Tony, Joey, and Ralphie, head for the roof, as Sal and others follow! The roof door flies open and boys burst onto the roof like gang busters! As they are racing across the roof, Sal, Bull Dog, and their crew, now at the rooftop door, are firing! Racing towards the edge, Tony, Joey, and Ralphie, have no options except they grab hands and jump.

On the corner the Sausage truck, with the huge rubber sausage on top, is parked. As the sausage sizzles, all of a sudden something hits the roof of the sausage truck. "What the hell?" The driver looks up, and then the back door of the truck flies open. Tony, Joey, and Ralphie, who are wearing the Al Pacino masks., "Al "Fucking" Pacino?" The driver with the three Al Pacino masks fly out the back-door as the sausage truck races off! Shots ring out. From the rooftop Sal, Bull Dog, and the others, open fire on, Tony, Joey, and Ralphie, in the speeding sausage truck. With Tony behind the wheel, Joey in the passenger seat, and Ralphie holding on for dear life, as rounds rip through the roof of the truck. Joey looks back, "they're shooting at us!" Tony slams the pedal to the metal, as he looks at Joey. Tony regrets that he was even born, "Life is not supposed to be like this, life is supposed to be." Joey, looking ahead, wildly points, and Tony is all confused, "What?"

Joey screams out, "WATCH OUT!" Tony looks ahead and screams! Standing right in front of the racing sausage truck is Rosalina, waving for the truck to stop. Next to her, on the sidewalk, is T-Bone with a shocked look on his face. "What the hell are you doing lady?" Rosalina waves like a crazed woman. "Stop! Stop!" Tony jerks the wheel as Joey and Ralphie scream. Within a whisker, the sausage truck just barely misses

Rosalina and T-Bone, and races up the street. As shots continue to ring out, the sausage truck hangs a hard right and disappears.

Still on the rooftop Sal looks at Bull Dog and the others. "I want them dead!" He turns and leaves as the others following, race along.

Tony is driving like a bat out of hell as Joey and Ralphie are scared out of their minds. "What are we going to do?"

Tony just shakes his head. "Drive! We're going to just keep driving!" Tony holds the wheel even tighter. They are now on the ramp to the Brooklyn Queens Expressway. The sausage truck roars up the ramp on onto the busy expressway. Tony just keeps driving with the intention of leaving New York.

CHAPTER SEVEN

The Only Thng The Boys Have In Life Is Themselves

A FTER HOURS OF DRIVING, and the truck goes across Pennsylvania, Ralphie starts to wonder, "Where the hell are we going to go?" Joey looks around, "I ain't ever been out of New York City!" Ralphie looks like he's about to cry. "I think we're lost!" Tony just wants to put a couple bullet through their heads for all the mess they got into.

"We ain't lost!"

'Then where are we?" As the truck cuts down into Kentucky, Tony tells Joey, "I think we are in Jersey!" A big bang comes from the truck, "What the hell?" The truck finally dies in Kentucky. Somewhere outside the State of Kentucky, they are pulled over by the side of the road, with steam coming from the radiator of the truck. Tony, Joey, and Ralphie, come out of the truck. Joey looks around and doesn't recognize his surroundings,

"I don't think this is Jersey?"

Ralphie, always being the stupid fuck that he is, turns to Tony, "this looks like Mars."

Tony looks around and smacks Ralphie upside the head, "Moron, it's fucking dark." Lightning lights up the sky and the guys scream, then suddenly heavy rain starts coming down. Tony and the guys race back into the truck. Tony looks up and realizes that they are getting soaked as the rain rushes through the bullet holes like a huge shower. The guys jump back out of the truck, as the lightning lights up the skies, they see an old barn in the distance. They look at each other, and then they race towards it. The rain starts to really pour down like buckets, and the boys have no choice. They open the barn doors and race in. They look around but they are in total darkness. Suddenly they hear, Moo! Joey starts to freak out.

'What the hell was that?'

"I think it was a cow." Ralphie replies, has he has his hands out, trying not to bump into anything. Tony, just really annoyed at both idiots and unable to see anything, starts to scream.

"Shut-up you guys! I'm trying to get the lighter."

Joey, all confused, continues to talk to Ralphie.

"You mean like a cow, cow?"

"Yea, like how now brown cow." Again they hear, Moo!

"You sure that wasn't a moose?" Tony has had enough, he keeps saying to himself, "How the fuck did me, TONY, end up with two fucking idiots like this?" He finally finds his lighter and lights it. They can finally see where they are and the guys were are standing right next to the cow.

Joey, being the closest to it, jumps away. "Whoa! I told you it was a moose!" Tony's lighter goes out and they are once again in darkness. Ralphie, still convinced, "It looked like a moose to me." Tony wishes there is some light so he can find Ralphie's head, so he can smack it.

"You idiot, that's a fucking cow!" Tony lights his lighter again and the cow is still there. There is also a lantern hanging on the wall close by. Tony grabs it and lights it. Joey starts to say to say something but Tony warns him. "Don't say anything!" Now, with a lantern lit, the inside of the old barn can be seen. The boys look around and see a pile of straw and bales of hay scattered about, with a corral for the cow and an old horse. They take their wet clothes off and make beds out of the straw. Tony and Joey are about to call it a night. Ralphie is dead asleep on his straw bed.

Joey looks at Tony, "I didn't really think that thing was a moose, I knew it was a cow." Tony smiles, and looks up and sees a huge hole in the roof. The rain has stopped by now.

"Of course, I knew you were kidding, Ralphie asleep?" Joey looks at Ralphie who is out cold.

"Like a baby. Wow, look at all those stars. I ain't seen stars in years."

"Yeah." Tony, lying on his bed, thinks for a moment. "This mess is my fault. I should have kept you guys out of it. I mean, life is not supposed to be like this, life is supposed to be—" All of a sudden Tony hears a big snore, he turns and looks at both Joey and Ralphie, snoring away like babies. Tony smiles, and then turns down the lamp. Tony finally falls asleep but not too long because he feels a shinny barrel of a double barrel shotgun nudging his cheek. Tony is dead asleep and starts to smile.

Joey starts to talk in his sleep, "Wow lady those sure are some hard."

They are woken up by a man's voice screaming. "Get your hands up peckerwoods!" Tony's eyes pop open and in horror Tony, Joey, and Ralphie, see Roscoe Washington, an African-American man in his sixties, wearing old sunglasses and dressed in overalls with a straw hat. He is standing there with the shotgun, and beside him is Daisy, a hot little Caucasian in her twenties, with long blonde hair wearing daisy dukes. Roscoe is getting really pissed off and screams again, "I'll shoot you!" The shotgun goes off and blows a hole in the roof of the barn. Daisy rolls her eyes and looks at Roscoe. "Lower Uncle Roscoe, lower!" He lowers the shotgun right at Tony, Joey, and Ralphie.

Tony lifts his hands, "Whoa, we." Roscoe points the gun again, "just because I'm blind you think you can sneak in here and try and hurt me and my niece?" Tony, Joey, and Ralphie look at Daisy and then they all look at Roscoe and right back at Daisy who gives them a mean look.

"I think these peckerwoods got guns Uncle Roscoe!"

"What the hell!"

Tony, Joey, and Ralphie, hit the dirt as a blast from the shotgun goes overhead. Tony flips out. "Are you crazy?" Joey looks at Tony and then at Uncle Roscoe, "you trying to kill us?" Uncle Roscoe shoots again and now Tony has to take a different approach because the more the boys get mad, the more shots come flying towards them.

"Okay, okay, you win, we will do whatever you want!"

Ralphie, scared for his life, puts his hands together as if he was praying, "Please don't shoot up!"

Joey follow suit, I'm too young to die!"

Daisy can't help but smile, "I guess I was wrong Uncle Roscoe, these peckerwoods seem safe."

"Well you can never be sure, especially when there is a fine black young woman like you around niece Daisy." Tony, Joey, and Ralphie, stare at Daisy, who smiles and then flips them the bird. The boys were confused, Daisy is not black, so she can't be his niece.

"Uncle Roscoe you're so sweet."

"Now you boys got five minutes to get off of my farm." Tony decides he's going to play along and try to reason with Uncle Roscoe. "But listen, we're traveling salesmen, and our truck broke down. We don't have any money, and we need a place to stay."

Ralphie jumps in, "yeah and see these other "salesmen" were going to kill us."

Roscoe is getting pissed, "WHAT?   Did you say kill?" Joey tries to help out Ralphie and jumps in, "No, no, he said ill, Joey starts to rap. "We be ill, when we're not chillin'... At here, your farm."

Roscoe puts his hand up, "I'm blind but I wish right now I was deaf, what the fuck was that?" Joey looks at Roscoe, "I was trying to rap. Please let us stay, we'll do anything."

"Is the boy retarded?"   Ralphie's eyes flash and he starts to say something, but Tony pops him in the belly with his elbow.

Daisy can't help but consider their offer. "You boys did say anything? You would do anything, right?"

Tony looks at Joey, then back at Daisy. "Yes anything."

Daisy looks at Tony and Ralphie who nod too. She then turns to Roscoe.

"Uncle Roscoe?"

'Yes Daisy?"

"'Member how you are always talking about be the Lord's helper and how we should help those in need?"

Uncle Roscoe drops his head, as Daisy looks at the guys with a "you owe me" look, as Roscoe nods.

"You're right niece."

"So, I was thinking maybe these boys could stay here until their truck is fixed up, and we do need help with all the chores. So maybe they could work for room and board."

Roscoe takes a breath.

"Well, it would be neighbourly, and it is planting time."

Tony, Joey, and Ralphie, shake their heads with their hands in prayer; they look up to the heavens. "Okay but after planting, they're going to have to go." Daisy takes Roscoe by the arm and starts walking him out of the barn.

"I'll get them settled Uncle Roscoe."

"You do that and I'll get back to my breakfast." Roscoe walks out of the barn. Joey looks at Ralphie and starts to rub his belly.

"Did he say breakfast?"

"I could eat a cow." Ralphie looks at the cow and licks his lips.

"Sorry." As Tony and the boys start to walk, Daisy turns to them and the sweetness is gone. "Not so fast losers." The boys look at Daisy as she stands there with her hands on her waist and ready to put them in their place. "We might be in a barn but I sure as hell wasn't born in one." Daisy takes at step closer. "I saw your truck. Those were bullet holes. Now I think you and I have to come to an understanding." Daisy smiles; "See poor blind Uncle Roscoe thinks I am his African-American niece, which is fine by me. What I did, who I did, or where I did it in the past, is nobody's business." Daisy stares down the guys. "I was here long before you guys, this has been a pretty good gig for me, if you guys mess it up..." Daisy grabs Joey by the shirt and pulls him close. "You'll sleep with the fishes. Got it?'

Tony and the guys nod. "Got it.'

"Good, now you boys are going to take over my chores around here. I say jump and you say?" Tony folds his arms, and Joey and Ralphie look at Daisy.

"Do I have to call Uncle Roscoe in here again, cause you know he wouldn't hesitate to put a bullet through you"? Joey and Ralphie shake their heads no. "Good. So I say jump and you say?"

Ralphie, always with a stupid remark says, "Up?" Tony just looks at Ralphie in shock and shakes his head. Ralphie has a look on his face like he's really thinking.

"What? You jump up. Oh no wait, frog! A frog jumps!" Joey in disbelief shakes his head, "Rope you dummy, you jump rope!"

Ralphie gives Joey a "look" but Tony can't take it anymore., "You fucking idiots it's HOW HIGH!   She says jump and we say how high, YOU IDIOTS!"

Joey looks at Daisy with pleading eyes. "Can we eat now?" Tony just shakes his head.

Early in the morning, outside the farmhouse, it looks just like a movie where Uncle Roscoe's farm sits outside the outskirts of Kentucky, with chickens on the porch and the dogs chasing the cat. The boys are sitting around a huge table in the dining room off the kitchen with Daisy and Roscoe. The table looks like a war zone. It's covered with empty plates, glasses, cooking utensils etc. Tony and the boys are stuffed from all they have eaten.

Uncle Roscoe, not seeing what a disaster the table is, asks, "Anyone want another biscuit?"

Tony puts his hands on his stomach, "No, no I think I will explode if I eat another bite."

Joey pretends he's not hungry but he can't keep it up. "Okay, just one more biscuit."

Tony and Ralphie look at Joey in amazement. "What? This is better than The Vegas." Roscoe looking up and just thinking out loud says to Joey.

"I met my fifth wife in Vegas."

"No not Las Vegas, Vegas Diner on eighty-sixth in Bensonhurst." WHAM! Tony catches Joey with a slap to the head. Uncle Roscoe is really confused, "Benson what?" Tony trying to cover up Joey's fuck up comes back with a comeback. "Yeah, Benson Uncle Roscoe, you look like that actor that played Benson on T.V." Joey was still rubbing his head from the smack that Tony just gave him, "Yea, yea, haven't you noticed the resemblance?"

"How could I? I'm blind." Ralphie thinks about it then nods. "Yea, yea he's right."

For a moment there's quiet at the table and then Ralphie couldn't help but ask, "Wait, you were married five times Uncle Roscoe?"

"That's right and they were all blondes."

Tony and the guys look at each other and Joey replies "Wow all blondes." Tony, knowing he's blind, is a little confused.

"Wait a minute, how could you tell they were blondes." Sensing something is wrong, Tony is quick to respond. "I thought you were blind?"

Roscoe laughs, "Of course I didn't know what colour their hair was. Boy, is you fellas dumb as dirt?"

Daisy puts her hand on Uncle Roscoe's shoulder, "Enough Uncle Roscoe, these poor boys would have to get up extra early to dance with your chickens." She starts to pick up the plates and clean up the mess the boys made. "You sure you boys had enough to eat?"

Joey rubs his stomach and leans back on in his chair, "That last biscuit did it for me." She raised her eyebrows, "That's good cause you're going to need all your energy." The guys look at Daisy and look at each other, "Why?"

"It's time for chores." Daisy reaches for something, "But first, got to put these on."

Daisy holds up three pairs of overalls. Tony has a look on of pain his face. "God, I hope I don't look as bad as you guys." Tony shakes his head. All three are wearing overalls, plaid shirts and straw hats. Joey looks at the other two boys up and down and shakes his head, "Well you do." Ralphie looks at Joey and Tony, "I kind of like these dudes." They look at him and just wonder where he came from. Daisy just looks at Ralphie, she smiles and just shakes her head.

CHAPTER EIGHT

Who Said Hard Work Doesn't Kill People?

THE SCENE ON THE FARM is like watching a comedy skit on T.V. Ralphie is being chased by a bunch of chickens, Daisy is watching all this. Tony and Ralphie picking up piles of smelly cow manure with big shovels. As the morning goes on Tony, Joey, and Ralphie, are covered in hay, feeding the cows. Joey, on a stool, is trying to milk a black cow with long horns. Roscoe and Daisy walk up to Joey and the cow bellows a moo. Uncle Roscoe is listening.

"What you doing fella?"

"I'm trying to milk this cow."

"What colour is that cow?"

"It's black."

"Does it have long horns?"

"Yeah real long ones."

"Does it have a bell around its neck?" Still sitting on the stool and milking, Joey looks at the neck of the cow.

"I don't see no bell."

Roscoe just shakes his head. "You ain't getting no milk."

"Hey, not yet but it's getting ready."

"You're a fool boy, that's a bull!" The bull bellows again and with excitement in its eyes, the bull looks at

Joey. Joey's eyes widen and he starts running as the big horny bull chases him. Tony and the boys start loading the hay bales into the upper part of the barn only to have it come falling back down. They are trying to pull the mule so they can plough but they are having no luck. Daisy yells at them to move it along. Joey pulls the plough while Tony and Ralphie hold it. The day is finally coming to an end and the boys are totally exhausted as they are getting ready for bed. Joey never worked so hard in his life. He turns and looks at Tony.

"I think I'm going to die."

"I've never worked so hard in my life." Ralphie chimes in, "That Daisy, she's the meanest lady I ever met!"

"You can say that again."

"That Daisy, she's—" Ralphie doesn't get to finish his sentence because Tony gets annoyed at him.

"Stop it, he didn't mean it literally." Tony looks at Joey, "Why do you do that? You know he's going to say it again. Sometimes I wonder about you."

"I was only busting his balls."

Tony has had enough. "Stop it all right. I just want to go to bed. I can't believe the mess we're in. I miss Donna." He looks at his hands, "My hands are covered in blisters. A man's hands ain't supposed to look like this. Don Luciano's hands, that's the way a man's hands are supposed to look like, manicured, nice, nothing like this." Joey and Ralphie don't know what to say. Ralphie tries to make Tony feel better, "Well at least we got it done."

"What's done?"

"The work." Joey agrees, "Yeah there can't be anymore work left." Tony thinks about their day and how much they accomplished., "Yea, you boys got a point I don't think there could be anymore. It doesn't make sense there." All of sudden Tony hears snoring and look over at Joey and Ralphie, and sees that they are both dead asleep. "Get some sleep fellas it's been a hell of a day." Tony lies down and quickly falls asleep.

The next morning, bright and early, they are awoken up by a loud ringing triangle. The boys are still in a dead sleep. Daisy rings the triangle again and the guys jump up scared out of their minds as Daisy continues to ring the triangle, and then she finally stops. Tony is annoyed and very tired and can't get the loud ringing loud sound out of his head.

"What the hell are you doing?"

"It's time for chores!" Joey rubs his eyes, "What the hell are you talking about?" Ralphie is still half asleep and can't believe his ears, "We did all the work yesterday!"

Daisy looks at Tony and the guys like they are crazy. "It's called chores fellas you do them every day."

Joey does not like what he hears, "No way!"

Ralphie is not doing this again, he was so exhausted from all the work they did yesterday that he is shocked at what she is telling them, "This much work could kill a person!"

Daisy just looks at the guys, "Do I have to have a little talk with Uncle Roscoe?"

Tony looks at Joey and Ralphie. "No." Reaching for their pants, Tony and the boys get dressed. Joey starts his day by getting ready to milk the cow. This time he is going to check and make sure it's a cow and not the crazy bull. Ralphie starts his day by getting the eggs. He's reaching for the eggs but gets attacked by the chickens. Daisy yells at him because he's getting all the chickens in an uproar. She turns and smiles at Tony and shows a little leg, Tony gets so distracted as he's riding the tractor that he loses control and smashes through the barn,

"Stupid bitch now why did she have to go and do that?"

She walks over to him and laughs, "what's the matter, you can't walk and chew gum at the same time?"

Tony jumps off the tractor, "why did you have to go and do that?" She smiles and starts to walk away, "I was a little bored and needed some excitement." Tony shakes some hay off of himself. "Yeah well go bother Ralphie and Joey I'm sure they will keep you occupied with all their stupidity?" She looks at him and orders him to get back to work. He gives her a dirty look and gets back on the tractor.

CHAPTER NINE

If You give Too Much Info You Qualify For Defeat

BACK AT THE OLD coffee shop Trinacria, that sits in the sun in Little Italy, Sal is sitting with at the poker table with Don Luciano playing a game, when his phone rings. Sal picks up the phone and listens to the person on the other end. His eyes widen and a serious and deadly look is on his face.

"Who is this?" He gets up and walks away from the noisy table. "A Friend?" He looks over at the table and motions Jimmy Two-Shoes to come over, as he covers the mouthpiece to the phone he says, "Trace this call." Jimmy Two-Shoes races to another phone and Sal continues listens. Looking around, Sal makes sure no one can hear him. "Well friend, you can bet your ass I am looking for a Tony, Joey and Ralphie." Sal smiles, "So where are those lovable boys?" Listening, Sal tries to lose it. "What? What? It doesn't matter where they are? You're calling the shots? Who the hell is this?" Sal takes a deep breath and continues to listen.

Daisy is sitting at the table back at the farm and smiles, as she's talking to Sal. "I'll tell you who the hell I am I'm the one that's hanging up on your ass!" Slamming down the phone, Daisy heads towards the door. In anger, Sal looks at the phone receiver, ready to smash it. Jimmy-Two shoes excitedly races up holding a piece of paper. "I got the address." Sal very happy and relieved he smiles and hangs up the phone.

Joey is feeding the sheep and notices one very peculiar looking sheep checking him out. He takes a step back and the sheep takes a step forward. He is not sure but he thinks he sees the sheep wink and then smile at him. He drops the feed bucket and runs for his life. As Tony comes around the corner, he finds Joey hiding behind a barrel.

"What the hell?" Joey motions for him to be quiet.

"I don't want her to find me."

"Don't worry, Daisy is making Ralphie's life hell." Joey looks around.

"I wasn't talking about her."

"Who the hell are you talking about?"

"Baa."

"What?"

Joey starts to lose it.

"It's what I call her. I don't know her name; she's a sheep."

"A sheep, what are you talking about." Joey grabs Tony and pulls him close.

"You have to listen to me, there's something wrong with this farm. All the animals are perverts." Tony pulls himself away from Joey's grasp.

"You're losing it Joey; I think you just need to get laid!"

"I was almost raped by a bull yesterday and today there is a sheep looking at me and she's got something on her mind."

Tony just shakes his head.

"You have finally gone insane." Tony walks away and leaves Joey with his sick theory as Joey pleads with him to stay.

"No, no, you can't leave." Suddenly Joey hears something behind him. He turns and is face to face, with the sheep! "No, no!" Joey turns and runs. He's running through the farm screaming for help with the horny sheep chasing him. Ralphie is getting dragged by a horse through piles of manure, as Daisy yells at him, and now a rooster has joined the chase with the sheep. Tony is just feeding the cows looking on like he is watching a comedy show and just shakes his head. He looks over and sees Daisy smiling at him. At this point, almost all of the animals are chasing Joey through the farm. Tony is just standing there wondering why is this bitch smiling at him me like she's up to no good and how in heavens name did he end up in this mess!

The day finally came to an end and the boys are dead tired. They lie on their bundles of hay and just try to get some sleep. Joey looks at Ralphie.

"We got to get the out of here!"

"It's not that bad."

"What the hell are you talking about? This is hell."

Tony doesn't want to hear it; he's had enough and can't take the boys anymore.

"Guys, just knock it off."   But they don't listen, Ralphie continues with Joey.

"Uncle Roscoe is a nice guy and the farm—" before he can finish Joey chimes in.

"Farm, this is Green Acres from hell you dummy!"

"Guys, really, I just want to—" Tony tries to get a word in but Joey just keeps on going.

"You try being a pin up doll for a sheep!" Ralphie just laughs,

"I was just saying—"

"You don't know what the hell you're talking about."

Ralphie starts to get steamed. "Well at least I know the difference between a bull and a cow!"

Joey jumps up, mad as hell. "Why, I ought to—"

Ralphie is up and ready to go, "Ought to what?"

That's it for Tony, who jumps up and grabs both Joey and Ralphie by the ears! The guys scream in pain. "Enough! Both of you are driving me crazy! Now knock it off!" Tony twists again, and Joey and Ralphie scream.

"Okay. Okay. Okay."

Tony lets go, and Joey and Ralphie are in pain and rub their ears. "I need some air.' Tony heads for the door, as Joey and Ralphie feel bad.

Ralphie tries to get Tony's attention, "Hey Tony."

And before he can say it Joey says it for the both of them, "We're sorry."

Tony turns and looks at the guys. "You're sorry, now, you're sorry? The biggest mistake I ever made was listening to you two. Now, my marriage is over before it ever got started, the men I wanted to work for want to kill me, and, and." Tony looks around in despair, "I am stuck in Kentucky!" Tony takes a breath. "The hell with it in the morning we are going back to New York and try to get to Don Luciano before Sal kills us, and try to work something out. Then, after that, I don't ever want to speak to you guys EVER again!" Tony just shakes his head and leaves, as Joey and Ralphie don't know what to say.

Stepping out into the night air, Tony takes a breath, and enjoys the silence, until out of nowhere he hears, "Yo Tony!" Tony looks and sees Daisy coming and he starts to just talk to himself.

"When it rains, it fucking pours."

"What?"

"I was just saying to myself how great it would be to see you." Daisy smiles as and she is now right in front of Tony.

"Oh, you're such a sweetie."

'I am, ain't I?" Daisy looks around.

"Where are those friends of yours?'

"You mean Joey and Ralphie? They're—" Daisy holds up her hand, cutting Tony off. "Listen, what I am about to say is Y.E.O." Tony doesn't understand what she is saying and Daisy just yells out, "Your ears only!"

"Oh... Y.E.O."

Daisy, smiles seductively at Tony. "Now, you and me, we could make a good team. We could take over this farm and the other ones," looking around Daisy makes sure no one is listening, "around here, and control the crops, cattle, everything. I got big plans. These hayseeds wouldn't know what hit them. We'd be rolling in the—"

"Hay?"

"I was thinking dough, but a toss in the hay with you wouldn't be bad either."

Tony smiles, "What's the split for me and my boys?"

"There ain't you and your boys no more, it's me and you or—"

"Or what?" Daisy now gets down to business with an evil smile.

"You know I wasn't born and bred on the farm Tony, I'm from Fourth and Flatbush."

"You were born in Brooklyn?"

'Born and bred, I called a friend of a friend and it seems a lot of people are looking for you guys."

"You made a call?"

"Don't get your shorts in an uproar, I didn't tell them you guys were here." Daisy gets as deadly as a cobra. "Now either you become my partner or your boys are kaput." Daisy leans closer to Tony and gives him a kiss. Once again Daisy is soft as a kitten, "I expect your answer in the morning." Daisy turns and leaves and Tony just shakes his head and walks towards the barn. Tony looks at the guys sleeping knowing this might be their last night of good sleep. As they are asleep in their beds, Tony starts to talk to himself. *Life is not supposed to be like this, life is supposed to be—*"

Suddenly, the roar of a deafening engine overhead startles the boys and they jump up wide awake. Blinding bright lights shine through the cracks in the barn as it shakes like it's in an earthquake!

Joey turns to Ralphie, "What the hell is going on?"

Ralphie practically in tears and ready to shit in his pants says, "Joey, I'm scared! I'm scared Joey!!!" Tony looks around then races for the door. Joey confused at what Tony is doing screams at him, "Where the hell you going?" Tony races out the door reluctantly Joey and Ralphie follow. Joey just looks at his watch and realizes it's two in the morning. They see a futuristic shiny Spaceship race across the sky.

Tony is in shock at what he just saw, "Wow! Did you guys see that?" Joey and Ralphie don't know what to say as they watch the spaceship slam into the cornfield with an explosion. Smoke and flames rise into the air. Tony looks at Joey and Ralphie very excitedly. "Come on guys!" Tony takes off towards the crash as the boys are frozen in their tracks.

Joey looks at in amazement, "No way am I going." Ralphie looks at Tony running and then back to Joey. "We can't let Tony go by himself." Ralphie takes off, leaving Joey behind in a state of shock. Joey, not really wanting to go, knows there is only one thing to do. "Heaven help us." Joey races into the cornfield and joins Tony and Ralphie who are standing at the edge of a smouldering crater looking down. Joey now sees what Tony and Ralphie are looking at, a shiny gold machine with plenty of handles, dials and instruments at the bottom of the crater. Joey says to Ralphie,

"What the hell is that?"

"I was just asking the same thing." Tony smiles. "That my friends, is the answer to all of our problems." Joey and Ralphie in amazement look at Tony. Tony looks at them like he just struck gold. "Ralphie go get the tractor."

"What the hell do we need the tractor for?"

Tony's smile just keeps getting bigger and bigger. "Just get the tractor Ralphie." Ralphie nods and heads towards the barn. He gets on the tractor and drives up to the crater where Tony and Joey are waiting. Tony and Joey, now covered in sweat, hook chains up to the machine. Ralphie, behind the wheel of the tractor with Tony and Joey pushing on the rear, pulls the strange machine out of the crater. Tony is gleaming. They get the machine in the barn near a pile of hay. The machine looks like pure gold and is covered with dials and handles, it looks like it almost has seats. Tony, Joey and Ralphie, covered in sweat and grime look at it. Joey is in awe, unable to make out what it is.

"What the hell is it?" Ralphie just as confused at Joey asks.

"I think it's some sort of alien espresso machine." Tony just shakes his head and just smacks Ralphie in the head.

"Alien espresso machine? Anyway it don't matter what it is once word gets out what it is we will be rich. Hell, that has to be real gold, it's got to be worth a million, at least!" Joey and Ralphie just have their dumb usual look on their face; Joey taps Ralphie on the arm.

"See Ralphie, that's why Tony is going to be huge someday, he knows things." Ralphie nods. "You're right Joey." Ralphie then looks at Tony. "Tony, you know things, things that only great men know."

Tony looks at Joey and Ralphie, and then takes a deep breath., "I owe you guys an apology I shouldn't get so mad at you. Listen, we'll sell this thing get back to New York." Looking at his two buddies Tony starts to smile, "we'll pay off Don Luciano and then you guys can crew up with me."

Ralphie and Joey are in shock, after all they had done and the whole mess they got Tony into he still wanted them to be part of his crew. Ralphie looks at Tony, "Really, you'd want us to hang with you?"

Joey put his hand on his heart and raises his right arm, "I promise I won't screw up anymore."

Tony just smiles and shakes his head, "Well don't make promises you can't keep but no matter what, it's us three." Tony sticks out his hand, "Forever." Ralphie and Joey stick out their hands in a baseball handshake. The guys touch hands and in sync say, "Forever," they shake on it.

* * * * *

OUTSIDE OF THE BARN the road lies empty. In the distance the the sound of a car coming can be heard. The big white shiny Escalade is making its way towards the barn. With the whole car full of smoke, T-Bone is on the phone while he smokes a fatty. He's arguing on the phone.

"I ain't that baby's daddy, he don't even look like me." T-Bone listens trying to convince the caller, "No, no way, that kids ears are the size of hubcaps. My ears are sexy." Suddenly T-Bone can't believe what he is seeing. Standing on the road is the Sheep that was after Joey with a bizarre "sexual" look on its face. T-bone quickly tosses the joint. "What the hell?" He slams on the brakes and the Escalade goes screeching past the sheep; he flies off the road hard into a ditch. With the air-bag inflated, T-Bone struggles to get out of the car. Barely standing T-Bone holds up the smashed cell-phone. "Great!" He tosses the phone down and that's when he sees the Sheep once again. "Hey you better get your woolly ass.," the sheep looks at T-Bone with love in its eyes and he knows something isn't right. "What are you looking at?" The Sheep lets out a strange baa and then charges T-Bone with love on its mind. There's only one thing T-Bone can do, he screams and runs towards Farmer Roscoe's barn in the distance.

T-Bone races for the door of the old barn; the horny Sheep is gaining fast. Punching the door open, T-Bone races into the barn. He just gets the door shut in time as the sheep slams into the outside of the door. Catching his breath, T-Bone wants to scream, but he sees a sleeping Tony, Joey and Ralphie on their straw beds. Trying to calm down, he then sees the golden machine shining in the moon light. Trans-fixed by the machine, he slowly walks toward it. Getting close, he looks at the machine and slowly reaches out to touch it. *"This thing must be worth millions!"* not realizing that Tony is right behind him.

"That thing is our thing."

T-Bone turns and is facing a now wide-awake Tony, Joey and Ralphie. Tony looks at T-Bone, "and what are you doing in here?"

Ralphie looks at Tony, "I got an idea what he's doing in here. He's trying to steal our space machine."

T-Bone does a double take at the machine, "Space machine?" Tony looks at Ralphie, then back at T-Bone. "He didn't say anything about space or a machine." T-

Bone raises his eyebrows, "I just heard him say it. Did this thing come from space? It would be worth billions then." Ralphie was surprised at what T-Bone said.

"Billions?" Joey just smacks Ralphie in the head. Tony tries to convince T-Bone that he misunderstood. "Nobody said anything about space. I'm going to ask you one more time, what are you doing here?"

T-Bone starts to get nervous., "I was on my way to a show. I was driving and suddenly this weird sheep"

"Sheep, did you say sheep?" Joey's eyes just widen and he looked around to see if the sheep is around.

"Yea, like baa, baa sheep. It's in the middle of the road, next thing I know, I'm in the ditch." T-Bone looks at the guys, "And then the sheep, it like tried to get up all in my business and I ended up in here."

Joey nods, "Yea that sheep, it's evil." Joey then looks at T-Bone, "You look familiar. What's your name?"

"T-Bone is the name, the rap world is my game." It hits Joey where he has seen T-Bone.

"Hey you were on a float at the San Gennaro Feast."

"That wasn't a float my brother, that was a stage."

'You're right. The world is a stage for you artists." Ralphie sees the resemblance.

"Oh my god, it's him, you got talent my friend."

"My voice that day was a little raw. I asked for hot water and honey, but—"

Joey compliments him, "I couldn't tell."

Ralphie looks at T-Bone, "Yeah me either but your rhymes, well, that's another story."   Tony couldn't believe this conversation was going on.

"Whoa! This isn't the weekly meeting of the lonely hearts club." Joey and Ralphie look at Tony. Tony looks at T-Bone and asks him again, "I'm going to ask you one more time, what are you doing here? Did someone send you?"

Suddenly they hear a man's voice creeping up behind them, "No one sent him Tony." The boys recognize the voice and in shock, turn and faced Sal, Bulldog, and Jimmy Two-Shoes.

T-Bone doesn't know what to think, standing next to them is Daisy, whose hands are tied and mouth is taped shut. Sal smiles at the boys, "but why don't you ask us what we're doing here?" Tony and the guys don't know what to say but T-Bone does. "Look, I don't give a—"

Sal holds up his finger to shut T-Bone up. T-Bone can't believe Sal just did that., "Oh, no you didn't! You didn't just lift your finger up to shut me—" Sal holds his finger up again. "You did it again!" Bulldog and Jimmy Two-Shoes jack rounds into their shiny Glocks.

Bulldog looks at Sal, "should I shoot the fucking idiot?" T-Bone looks at Tony with a look of horror on his face. "Why the hell didn't you tell me they had guns?"

"I don't even know who you are!" Joey tries to seize the opportunity. "Hey, it's good to see you guys. We were just getting ready to call you, right Ralphie?" Ralphie doesn't pick up on what the hell Joey is talking about, then again, Ralphie doesn't pick up on anything that anyone tries to tell him. "Why would we call them, they were trying to kill—" Both Tony and Joey put their hands over Ralphie's mouth.

Tony looks over at Sal with a nervous smile, "Sal, it's good to see you, we have the money." Sal looks at the guys then looks at the old looking machine. "It looks like you got more than that."

Jimmy Two-Shoes has a smile from ear to ear, "Whoa! You thinking what I'm thinking?" Sal gives Jimmy a dirty look, "No one does the thinking but me."

Bulldog walks around the machine and is admiring it. "I bet the whole thing is made out of gold!"

Sal smiles a big smile. "That's what I was thinking. I was also thinking, it's time to;" The smile disappears from Sal's mouth. "Blast them!" The boys get a look of fear in their eyes and put their hands up over their heads to try and take cover but suddenly there's banging on the door, its Uncle Roscoe.

"Daisy! Daisy!" The door flies open., Uncle Roscoe enters with shot-gun up and ready to blast. Sal, Bulldog, and Jimmy Two-Shoes, point their guns at Uncle Roscoe. "Daisy, I know you're in here with them boys, fornicating, and doing all sorts of nasty things!" Quickly thinking, Tony calls out to Uncle Roscoe. "Daisy's not here Uncle Roscoe!"

"I might be blind boy, but I ain't stupid." Sal, Bulldog, and Jimmy-Two Shoes, look at each other and put their guns down as Uncle Roscoe continues walking into the barn. "I know you young people got the "itch," the itch that got to be scratched. Now, I know she's in here!" Tony looks at Sal, but Sal shakes his head no way! "I'm not leaving! I know she's out here and you boys have been taking-'old-one-eye' to the optometrist with my sweet little niece!" Sal knows there's nothing he can do and though he doesn't want to he pulls the tape off Daisy's mouth but motions everyone to be quiet!

"We weren't doing nothing Uncle Roscoe."

Uncle Roscoe smiles, "I knew you were out here!"

"We were just talking that's all." Suddenly there is a noise from above and everyone looks up, except for Uncle Roscoe of course. On the roof near the hole, is the crazed sex-starved sheep, which is looking down on everyone! BAAA! BAAA!

Uncle Roscoe hears it, "It's that evil perverted sex crazed sheep!" Uncle Roscoe lets go with a blast from the shotgun and all hell breaks loose. Sal and his gang grab Daisy and dive for cover, as Uncle Roscoe fires another blast.

As the sheep dives from the roof, Daisy screams. Tony, Joey, Ralphie and T-Bone, with nowhere to hide, race towards the machine. They jump on the machine, trying to hide, as the crazy sheep lands with a thud and lets out a sex starved BAAA!!! Uncle Roscoe turns his head wildly, "I hear the bastard!!!"

Hay flies and everyone starts yelling, trying to hide, as Uncle Roscoe keeps spinning around and firing at the now racing sheep!

Sal, getting really annoyed screams, "Blast the old man! Blast the old man!" A blast hits right near Sal, Daisy, Bulldog and Jimmy-Two Shoes, and they dive for cover.

Tony, trying to get the situation under control, starts to scream, "No, don't shoot. He's blind. Uncle Roscoe please stop shooting."

"You people are crazy!" T-Bone is regretting running into the barn and getting himself in this mess.

Tony is pleading with Uncle Roscoe, "Uncle Roscoe you have stop shooting."

Joey is hiding and praying for his life, "I don't want to die!"

Ralphie looks at Joey with the same fear in his eyes, "Me either!!! I'm too." Trying to duck down, Ralphie grabs a handle. Suddenly, a winding noise is heard, the dials start to spin, and smoke starts to come out. Ralphie is all freaked out and has no clue what's going on. "What the hell, hey guys I think something is going on here." Ralphie tries to get the other guys attention but can't; they are fixated on trying to not to get shot by Uncle Roscoe, who's waving the gun around!

Tony keeps yelling, "Stop shooting Uncle Roscoe!"

Jimmy Two-Shoes is scared and looks at Sal, "you sure you want me to blast him boss?"

T-Bone looks at Jimmy with fear in his eyes, "That crazy old bastard is going to kill us all!"

Uncle Roscoe is determined to get that sick, perverted sheep. "I'll kill ya, you horny good for nothing sheep!" And he continues to shoot.

Ralphie knows that the machine should not be smoking like this and still tries to get the attention of the guys, "Fellas I don't think this is too good." Ralphie grabs a hold of Joey's sleeve as more smoke starts to fill the air. "Hey Joey!"

Joey is scared that he's going to get hit with a flying bullet and doesn't pay any attention to Ralphie. "Not now Ralphie."

But T-Bone notices and starts to turn around and more dials start to spin. "What the hell" A huge loud bang is heard and suddenly, some gold bars starts to slide out and slam down around Tony and the guys. The noise is so loud that Sal, Daisy, and the others, look, and it even stops Uncle Roscoe in his tracks. The boys and T-Bone are impressed by the machine, now that it's firing up, even the sheep stops and looks at it. More smoke bellows out and the machine starts to vibrate.

Tony, not knowing if it's going to explode, looks in shock. "What the hell is happening?"

Ralphie, finally relieved that he got their attention, looks at Tony, "I tried to tell you guys."

Joey is still scared; he thinks he's going to die either way, whether it's the bullets or the machine. "I don't think this is going to be good."

Uncle Roscoe wants to know what is going on and lowers his shotgun. "What the hell is happening?"

Sal, Daisy, Bulldog and Jimmy-Two Shoes stand, and in amazement, look at the machine.

Jimmy looks at Sal. "Should I blast them boss?"

Sal is annoyed and a little nervous because he doesn't know what's happening, "Shut up you moron, you just want to blast anyone!" As the machine starts to shake more, a wind begins to blow around the barn.

Uncle Roscoe, unable to see, feels helpless and a little nervous, "What the hell is going on?" The sound is getting louder and louder and the machine is vibrating more and more. The wind starts whipping around faster and faster and the smoke is getting thicker and thicker.

T-Bone looks at Tony. "Are you thinking what I'm thinking?"

Tony just looks at the machine, "Yep! We're screwed!" With a blast of blue lighting, the barn fills with electricity. The blast knocks Uncle Roscoe, Sal, Daisy, Bulldog, Jimmy Two-Shoes, and even the sheep, flying backwards. Tony, Joey, Ralphie, and T-Bone disappear, with the gold machine into thin air. Sal is dazed and sees that Joey and the others, with the machine, have disappeared.

Uncle Roscoe crawls out from under a pile of hay with Daisy by his side. "What the hell just happened?"

Bulldog and Jimmy-Two Shoes, who land in a huge pile of manure, try to crawl out. "That's it! Someone is going to die!" Bulldog just wants to put a bullet through someone.

Sal is still confused and now really annoyed at Bulldog. "No one is doing nothing until I find out what the hell is going on here." Sal looks at a smoky burnt empty spot where the machine, Tony, Joey, Ralphie, and T-Bone had been.

CHAPTER TEN
The Flight Through Time

FLYING THROUGH TIME, IMAGES of the present and past fly by, as sparks and flames burn. Of course Tony, T-Bone, Joey, and Ralphie, are screaming their lungs out. Suddenly, there's a loud explosion, as the machine starts the fall. With a look of horror the guys look downward and scream as the machine begins to rapidly fall. They finally hit the ground. They land in Rome 70 A.D., The Coliseum on a gorgeous sunny day. The boys in the machine hit the hard ground in a huge puff of dust. As the dust clears, they can't believe what they are seeing, all the citizens of Rome sitting in the famous Coliseum, who can't believe their eyes. Even the lions and tigers that were fighting the Gladiators just stop and stare at the machine, as the boys tumble off the machine. They are blinded by the dust and the guys are crawling around like a bunch of blind mice.

Tony tries to speak but Joey beats him to the punch. "What's going on? I can't see a thing!"

T-Bone, scared exclaims, "I'm blind, I'm blind!"

The dust clears and Ralphie, finally getting the dust out of his eyes, can't believe what he is seeing. "Hey fellas I think there's something really wrong here, this doesn't look like New York!"

Tony, T-Bone, and Joey, wiping the dust out of their eyes, finally can see. Looking around, Tony is in shock. "No shit you idiot. Tell me what gave it away, the Tigers and Lions or the Gladiators? Because if you ask me, New York isn't any different!" He gives Ralphie a sarcastic look and smacks him on the head. "Okay, what's going on here? Is this some kind of joke?"

Joey looks around and then smiles. "Wait this looks like that Russell Crowe movie, Spartacus. We're on a movie set!"

T-Bone looks at Joey like he's nuts., "Spartacus, what are you, retarded? The movie was called Gladiator. Tony these boys are a little on the slow side, what the fuck are you doing hanging out with them?"

Tony just shakes his head because T-Bone said the one word that will flip Ralphie out and with that thought Ralphie flips out. "Whoa! Stop right there."

Joey looks at T-Bone and gives him a "no you didn't" look. "Now you did it! He goes crazy if you use that word." T-Bone is confused, "Gladiator? What the hell is wrong with that?"

"No, the other word, the one that starts with "R"

"You mean retard?" Ralphie sees red! "Now I have to believe that you don't know how offensive that word is, because if you did and you—"

Tony puts up his hand and shuts the boys up. "Hey fellas." Tony notices that a group of Gladiators with the Tigers and Lions are now heading their way.

Ralphie is not looking at Tony, "Not now Tony, I'm trying to teach Mr. Ham-bone a lesson here."

"Ham-Bone? The name is T-Bone and if there is any teaching around here"

Joey looking out at the still stunned spectators, shakes his head. "Where's the director of this movie? These extras in the stand are the worse."

Ralphie and T-Bone are still going at it. "It sounds to me like you are looking for a fat lip!" T-Bone is now nose to nose with Ralphie, "Sounds to me like you want to meet the gun show." T-Bone flexes his muscles as neither guy notices that the Gladiators are getting closer and closer.

Tony is getting nervous as they are getting closer, "Hey guys knock it off!" Joey, finally notices the oncoming Gladiators. "Wow! These Gladiators look right out of central casting, those swords look real."

Meanwhile Ralphie and T-Bone are still nose to nose. Ralphie is pissed,

"It looks like you are about to get a five-finger invitation to the black and blue party!"

"Oh yea, well allow me to bring something to the party, a knuckle sandwich." Both men have their fists up like old Victorian fighters as a Gladiator approaches Tony with a sword held high. "Wait that sword is real." Tony ducks, as the sword swung by the gladiator just misses him.

A lion licks his lips hungrily and eyes Joey., "That lion is looking at me like I'm a big pile of my mama's beef *braciole.*"

Tony ducks again as the Gladiator once again attacks, "Enough of this nonsense." The crowd roars as Tony takes out the Gladiator with a haymaker and then a swift kick to the balls! The Gladiator drops his sword and screams in pain.

A strange silence falls over the Coliseum. Tony, Joey, Ralphie, and T-Bone, are now circled by the rest of the Gladiators and lions. Tony looks at the crowd, then at the

Gladiators, and then back to his pals. "Okay, they want some acting they're going to get some." He then takes a deep breath and steps away from Joey and holds up his sword. "I am Maximus!"

Joey shakes his head., "Russell Crowe got an Oscar for that line."

Tony gives Joey a warning look. "I said I am Maximus!"

Joey nods. "Oh, I get it! Strength and", T-Bone now gets what Tony is doing, "Honour... Strength and Honour! That's right!" Watching in the stands is the noble leader of all of Rome, Caesar. Sitting with him is the one and only the hot, sexy, Queen of Egypt, Cleopatra. Cleopatra locks eyes with T-Bone, she quivers and makes a growling sound like a beast. T-Bone just winks and kisses his guns as Cleopatra swoons and falls out of her chair.

Ralphie noticing, smiles, "I think someone is sweet on you!" T-Bone smiles at Tony, who is now in full command, looks at his pals. "It's time to unleash a good old Mulberry Street beat down." Joey, Ralphie, and T-Bone, scream and start throwing vicious rights, lefts and haymakers! Gladiators go flying! They spin, kick and belly bump other Gladiators. Swords are strewn everywhere. The crowd's screaming goes wild. Joey has gotten the attention of the lions and tigers, which look at him like he's a Mirage buffet.

"Down, in the name of Caesar Milan the Dog Whisperer, I say." He slowly picks up a whip from the ground and snaps it. "In the name of Siegfried and Roy, come to papa. *Aueviderzen, apple strudel, danka, Heinekin*, NOW!"

The lions suddenly jump into a chorus line and then start to run in a circle. The crowd goes crazy again. Tony, Ralphie, Joey, and T Bone, with swords held high, look triumphantly into the stands. Flowers and coins, from the crowd start pelting our unlikely heroes.

Brutus a mousey looking guy, races up to next to Caesar, "These men must be taken care of Caesar; they are riling up the masses and the contraption there." Brutus points to the Time Machine, "I smell danger." Caesar looks at Brutus,

"But the people adore them."

"Then spare them their lives but they must be treated as they truly are, SLAVES!"

Caesar nods as everyone waits. He finally gives definitive thumbs up and the crowds roar, as guard's race in and grab Tony, Joey, Ralphie, and T-Bone, and drag them away! Tony, Joey, Ralphie, and T-Bone, being dragged by their hair, arms and legs, down the stone halls by the Guards. They are inside the dark Coliseum and of course Joey still thinks he's still on a movie set. "Wow, this almost looks real." Ralphie also amazed at the set., "Yea, this is amazing CGI."

T-Bone looks at Tony. "What the hell is going on here?"

"That's what I am trying to figure out." The guys pass by prison cell after prison cell. The prisoners come running up to the gate, begging to be let out, while other skinny prisoners are whimpering in the corners of their cells. Some prisoners are fighting off rats and maggots and some poor souls are not fighting at all. Inside a dark cell door, the head guard, a rough looking big guy, grabs the rusted keys from his pockets.

Tony and the guys try to bust free but the guards quickly subdue them and the Head Guard opens the cell door.

"In you go!" With one hand he tosses them all in the cell. They hit the stone wall with a loud thud. The guards laugh with pleasure as the Head Guard locks the cell door. Then the guards march off. The boys are now shaken they stand and dust themselves off. They look around in horror except for Ralphie.

"This looks a lot like Resident Evil level four or maybe level five."

Joey smacks him on the head, "shut up Ralphie.' Joey looks around, "Obviously this is not the work of the brilliant director Ridley Scott. This is some "B" level piece of crap action movie."

Ralphie shakes his head. "No Joey no, this smells of "video game movie", like ya know, Tomb Raider, but nowhere near the iconic Lara Croft."

Having heard enough Tony explodes, "Shut up the both of you! I have to have time to think."

Joey continues as if Tony said nothing. "Whatever the hell this is, it sucks. If I had an agent I would call him. They can't treat people like this!"

Ralphie trying to give them the benefit of the doubt, "they can if we are extras."

All of a sudden something moves under the pile of straw in the corner. The guys look at each other and then dash to the other corner in fear. Slowly a decrepit, brittle, old man, crawls out of the stall. Maximus has a beard down to his knees and an old cane made of human bone.

"Hello fellas, Maximus Padius the name and dancing is my game." Suddenly he breaks out into a dance that strangely resembles a Charleston. T-Bone looks in shock, "Wow that is weird." Tony confused at what he's talking about.

"That he's dancing the Charleston?"

"No, that his name is Maximus Padius, Maxi Pad, get it?" Tony just shakes his head as Maximus finishes his dance and bows. "That was great old man." Maximus extends his wart and feces covered hand. T-Bone smiles and backs up.

"I see you fellows are the new guys on the block." Joey just shakes his head and starts to look around.

"Where the hell is the director?"

"You mean Caesar, Caesar wouldn't be caught dead down here." Tony gives Maxi Pad a double take, "Caesar, yeah right." Tony looks around. "Maybe we did land on a movie set." Ralphie still convinced it's not a real movie, looks at Joey.

"Like I told ya, this is some sort of video game movie."

"Well this had better be a studio flick."

Maximus having no clue what the boys are talking about looks at them and just raises his eyebrows, "Wow, you fellas are sure strange." Suddenly he sees a white mouse and dashes for it. He catches it by the tail and lifts it up. "Anybody want a bite?" Tony and guys look at Maximus in horror. "I'm just kidding." Maximus lets the mouse go then see sees a huge cockroach.

He grabs it and gobbles it down. T-Bone turns his face in disgust, "I think I'm going to be sick."

Tony is not liking this movie at all. "What kind of movie is this?" They all just stare at Maximus. Tony, Joey, Ralphie and T-Bone, are scared out of their minds, and are huddled together on the far wall across from Maximus, who is now doing yoga, and is in the Warrior position.

Tony, the first to realize it, looks at the boys., "This isn't a movie set." Joey, Ralphie, and T-Bone, nod quickly in agreement. "Somehow that machine sent us back in time." Joey, Ralphie, and T-Bone, once again nod quickly in agreement. "We got to find that machine and get the hell out of here!"   Again, the guys nod in agreement.   Suddenly the guards appear out of the darkness with three large bowls. They reach the gate of the cell and bang loudly. Tony and the guys jump up and scream. The guards slide the bowls on the floor, into the cell. Maximus grabs a bowl and starts to eat some evil looking slop, and looks at the Head Guard.

"Proximo looking good, you've lost some weight. How are the kids?"

"The youngest is a hand full."

"The youngest always are."

Tony steps up to the Head Guard., "Listen, we shouldn't be here. We should be in Kentucky, you know America, somehow."

The Head Guard slaps Tony across the face. "Don't talk to me slave." He and the other guards then turn and leave.

Tony can't believe what happened. "Why the hell did he slap me, he slapped me!"

Maximus doesn't want to hear it. "You're lucky he didn't cut your ear off." Maximus shows him that he has no ear. "You better eat up before it gets cold." The guys look into the bowls. Some sort of meat can be seen but it's covered in flies. Tony looks at it in disgust and pushes it away, "Hell no, I'm not eating that. My dog wouldn't even eat that."

Maximus looks up from his bowl. "Dog? That was last night."

T-Bone has had enough of this. "That ain't right."

"Right or wrong you guys better eat, you'll need your strength to fight."

Joey stares at Maxi Pad, "What are you talking about?"

Ralphie, not liking what he hears, also stares at Maxi Pad, "Fight?"

T-Bone looks at them and says, "I'm not fighting, my raps are my weapons!"

"You're in the Coliseum, that's all we do." Tony takes a breath, "look we just want to head home, how you get out of here?"

"No one has ever escaped from the Coliseum. There's only one way out." Maximus points to the front of cell as Guards go by carrying a dead man. Tony, Joey, Ralphie, and T-Bone, take a deep breath, and look at each other.

Ralphie looks at Tony, "it's like being in the mob, and you only get out when you are six feet under!" Joey looks at Ralphie, "that's the smartest thing you said today." Ralphie has a proud look on his face.

* * * * *

LATER THAT NIGHT, THEY are all in the cell in their corners and all are fast asleep. Ralphie is in a corner, dead asleep, unaware that Maximus is cuddling with him. Inside the dark hallways of the Coliseum the sound of a pair of silk slippers shuffle on the ground, they are covered with crystal and jewels. All of a sudden, they stop in front of the cell. A soft delicate hand reaches through the bars and lovingly strokes the cheek of a sleeping T-Bone.

T-Bone is talking in his sleep, "Eminem has nothing on me." The hand, impatient, slaps him. T-Bone screams and jumps up in fright. His scream wakes up everyone.

Joey looks over around, "What the hell?" Ralphie comes to and realizes he is being spooned by Maximus; he pushes the old man off him. T-Bone sees Cleopatra covered in a magenta veil with the Head Guard behind her. The Head Guard opens the cell and points to T-Bone.

"The Queen wishes you to come with her." Cleopatra winks at T-Bone.

T-Bone smiles and winks at her., "I hear ya baby, sounds like you need a booty call."

T-Bone starts to head out but Tony grabs his arm. "Hey it's cool, a booty call and all, but we got to get out of here."

T-Bone smiles at Tony. "Trust me, when I get done with her, she'll do anything we want."

T-Bone steps out with Cleopatra and the Head Guard who shuts the cell door. T-Bone looks back at the guys. "Don't wait up for me." He shoots a peace sign to Tony and the guys, as he walks down the hall with Cleopatra on his arm.

Tony looks at the boys. "What kind of "Back to the Future" crap is this? I mean a time machine, it's not possible."

Ralphie looks at Tony, "well, if you think about it, the variable speed that we were using to time travel means Einstein's equation of relativity is correct. We are living proof that E does equal MC squared."

Both Joey and Tony stare at Ralphie with utter amazement.

"I stand corrected Ralphie, that has to be the smartest thing that ever came out of your mouth!"

*   *   *   *   *

T-BONE AND CLEOPATRA WALK down the dark hallway. Suddenly she turns and to the Head Guard. "You are dismissed!"

The head guard bows to his Queen, "Yes your highness!" The Head Guard turns and marches off.

T-Bone likes the power she has, "Well, well, I think."

Cleopatra grabs T-Bone and slams him against the wall. "You like it rough huh?" Passion overwhelms

Cleopatra and she goes crazy and starts attacking T-Bone. T-Bone tries to keep up but Cleopatra is all over him kissing, biting and gyrating like a mad-woman.

T-Bone grabs her hair and it comes off in his hand. He is in shock looks at Cleopatra and notices something. He reaches up and pulls off her veil. He sees that "she" is really a "he" with slight stubble. It's not Cleopatra at all that he had been kissing, it's her man servant, No-Testicle-Us, a flamboyant gay eunuch. T-Bone jumps back in fear and panic as No-Testicle-Us smiles and steps forward. "No, no that's okay, bearded and freaky is not really my thing!" T-Bone turns and starts to run down the hallway. Suddenly out from the dark, the real Cleopatra steps out. It's lights out for T-Bone when Cleopatra hits him with a small club.

Inside her bedroom, a spacious, richly decorated bedroom, in the Roman Temple named, Skank-U-Tus, lays the sleeping face of T-Bone, as once again a delicate hand strokes his face. "Jay-Z my ass!" Suddenly T-Bone's eye's pop open. "The last time this happened, things didn't work out so well." T-Bone sees that the real Cleopatra is straddling him with a big smile. T-Bone looks around and sees No-Testicle-Us is on the other side of the room doing a fan dance. He then looks at Cleopatra. "You're a woman right, Va-Jay-Jay and all, right?"

No-Testicle-Us smiles and points to Cleopatra, "There's no one more woman than Cleopatra!"

Cleopatra eyes T-Bone like a steak. "I can just eat this fine Nubian specimen whole," Grinding on T-Bone Cleopatra smiles. "And his "man muscle" seems as big and strong as the Nile!"

T-Bone smiles and looks at Cleopatra, "you are one fine piece of ass my Cleopatra Jones. It's time for a one hundred per-cent real beef T-Bone special!" T-Bone is up and he and Cleopatra lock eyes and start to circle each other. Both growl and licking their lips as No-Testicle-Us is now doing an insane dance with scarves. Suddenly Cleopatra lets out a blood curdling scream and flies in the air.

T-Bone with a look of horror in his eyes tries to back up but is too slow. "Help Me! She is going Angelina Jolie on my ass!" Cleopatra lands on T-Bone knocking him onto the bed. She then flips him over and starts riding him like a bucking bronco. "Oh My God, what the hell is going on?"

Seeing red, T-Bone bucks Cleopatra off and stands up. "That's it now you're going to meet my "really big" little friend!" T-Bone unzips his pants and all of a sudden there is a substantial thud! Cleopatra and No-Testicle-Us look down and gasp, then T-Bone looks down, "Sons of a bitches, my Chronic!" Cleopatra and No-Testicle-Us look at each other and then at T-Bone. "You guys don't know what Chronic is?" They both shake their heads no. "I am going to rock your world." T-Bone breaks into a huge smile. With a puff of smoke off a huge joint T-Bone lies in bed with an exhausted but completely satisfied and stoned to the bone Cleopatra. With her black wig off Cleopatra is completely bald as a cue ball! T-Bone does a double take. "Whoa! Britney Spears! Let's put the wig back on."

Cleopatra takes a huge hit. "So you like that huh? Well, I know where you can get more." Cleopatra smiles and starts grinding once again on T-Bone. "See there is a machine, a huge machine that." Cleopatra gyrates even more. "Damn, you're like a machine. Speaking of a machine, if you help me find that gold machine" T-Bone acts like he's smoking a joint, Cleopatra goes even faster. "Damn girl, slow down, you're going to break my leg." He grabs a hold of Cleopatra, "Bitch chill! I need to get my boys, get that machine and get the hell—"

No-Testicle-Us pops his head out from under the covers at the bottom of the bed. "Now that's a spicy meatball!" No-Testicle-Us kisses his fingers and jumps out of bed. T-Bone has a look of fear which turns to all out horror when No-Testicle-Us bends over to pick up a fan. The sound of a record needle scratching across a record goes inside T-Bones head. Everything stops. "No-Testicle-Us! Oh my god, my man! You got no balls!" T-Bone jumps out of bed, "This is way too freaky deakey for me. I'm getting off the freak train right now!" Cleopatra and No-Testicle-Us just stare at T-Bone. "First we got to get my peeps. Second, we got to find that machine and third, I have to get home." T-Bone is dead serious now. "I never thought I would say this, but it's time to put the Chronic down and get moving." Cleopatra and No-Testicle-Us follow T-Bone out the door.

* * * * *

MEANWHILE AT THE SENATE floor, Brutus and his crew stand in the famous Rome Senate, looking in awe at the Time Machine sitting before them. "This weird contraption is the secret to the power that those idiots in the Coliseum showed today." Brutus touches the Time Machine. "It could be useful in our plans for dear Caesar."

"But what kind of machine is it?" Brutus shakes his head, "Some sort of a flying thing machine or something."

"But sir, if we don't know anything about it, shouldn't we leave it alone"

Rolling his eyes, Brutus has heard enough. "If we don't know anything about it, shouldn't we leave it alone?" one of his men sarcastically asks.

Brutus goes ballistic. "How dare you question my authority? Caesar is just a peasant with a crown. He knows nothing of real power." Suddenly the sounds of footsteps are heard coming and Brutus and his crews hide. Slowly the Soothsayer, an ancient looking man who walks with a ornate cane, comes into the room. He slowly reaches out and strokes one of railings on the machine and smiles. "I know you're there, come out now." Brutus and his crew slowly come out as the Soothsayer steps onto the machine.

"Do you know what this device is?"

"All I know is that if I can figure out its power." Brutus smiles, "you will be at my side as I rule the known world."

The Soothsayer now smiles and reveals a mouth full of ugly black teeth. "Climb aboard old great one." Brutus carefully steps onto the Time Machine as the Soothsayer shuts his eye and mumbles an ancient prayer. "With the power of Zeus, I summon…" The Soothsayer, with his eyes still shut, reaches out and twists two knobs. Suddenly a winding noise is heard, and all the dials start to spin and smoke starts to come out. Suddenly gold bars starts to slide sliding out and slam slamming down around the Soothsayer and Brutus! More smoke bellows out and the machine starts to vibrate. The machine starts to shake more and now the wind starts to blow around the Senate, and Brutus' crew looks on in amazement. The sound is getting louder and louder and the machine is vibrating more and more. The wind starts whipping around faster and faster and the smoke is getting thicker and thicker! With a blast of blue lightening, the Senate fills with electricity, KA-BOOM!   The machine disappears.

* * * * *

BACK AT THE BARN, Sal, Bulldog, and Jimmy Two-Shoes, are still staring where the Time Machine went. Daisy, also curious, joins the search with them.

Jimmy looks at Sal, "Sal, I think—"

Sal puts his hand up to shut him up., "How many times do I have to say that NOBODY does any thinking around here but me, YOU GOT THAT!" Jimmy Two-Shoes scared quickly, nods and then looks at Bull Dog who just shrugs.

Daisy smiles and hooks her arm around Sal's. "You can do all my "thinking" anytime you want."

Meanwhile Uncle Roscoe tries to reload his shotgun desperately checking his pockets for shells. "I heard that you lying little incubus. When I find my shells, I'll send you and those evil friends of yours all to hell in a hand basket." All of a sudden the earth starts to shake.

Jimmy Two-Shoes looks at Bulldog, "I don't like this."

Bulldog looks around. "Not again!"

Daisy tries to hide behind Sal as Sal wildly starts firing his gun.

Jimmy-Two Shoes and Bulldog run for cover as Uncle Roscoe tries to figure out what is going on. "Whoever you are you better pray I don't find my shells!"

Smoke starts filling the air, then lightening, and sure enough a loud THUD! The time machine is back with Brutus and the Soothsayer. Sal with a look of shock on his face can't believe what he is seeing. "Who the hell are you?!"

Brutus just looks at him. "The question is who are you?"

"Who am I, "I" is none of your business." Sal points his gun at Brutus and the Soothsayer as Jimmy Two-Shoes and Bulldog join him.

Bulldog is ready to shoot someone, "what, you guys trying to be smart with us?"

"You are in the presence of greatness and soon to be the leader of all the Roman Republic." Sal, Jimmy Two-Shoes and Bulldog mouths drop!

"You're Caesar?" Jimmy Two–Shoes smiles at Sal with widened eyes, "The one and only Caesar?" Jimmy Two-Shoes and Bulldog drop down to one knee. "It's an honour to meet you."

Brutus can't believe what he is hearing. "Caesar, I am Marcus Junius Brutus, you may call me Brutus."

Farmer Roscoe's head snaps, and he approaches Brutus. "Brutus? Hey, ain't you the fella that killed Caesar?" Farmer Roscoe once again reaches for shells.

"Damn! Where are my shells?"   Sal, Bull-Dog, and Jimmy Two-Shoes, lift their guns! Sal gives the order, "Shoot the rat!" They are all out of bullets.

Brutus not impressed, looks at Soothsayer, "Get us the hell out of here!"   The Soothsayer starts spinning knobs. The earth starts to shake and smoke starts to fill the air. Sal, Jimmy Two-Shoes, and Bulldog, fire, as Daisy starts to screams. With lightening speed, the Time Machine disappears and once again Sal, Jimmy Two-Shoes, Bull-Dog, Daisy, and Uncle Roscoe, are blown backwards. The Time Machine re-appears on the senate floor. Brutus jumps off and yells to his crew, who are in shock. "Quickly we have no time! The intruders must die!" Brutus and his crew race out of the Senate.

* * * * *

INSIDE THE UPPER LEVEL of the Coliseum, in the middle of the night, T-Bone, Cleopatra, and No-Testicle-Us, peer around a corner; they see servants scurrying and guards stationed at every pillar down a hallway. Straight off some Rambo movie, T-Bone points first to his eyes and then points down the hallway, signalling Cleopatra and No-Testicle-Us, to look down the hall. But they misunderstand, and start looking at T-Bone, with only one thing on their minds, Sex. "No not now. We got to get my peeps and then el Chronic." T-Bone acts like he is smoking weed. "Then sexy time!"

Cleopatra and No-Testicle-Us smile, and she looks at T-Bone.

"Yea Boi!" T-Bone puts his finger up to his lips, "Quiet." He signals No-Testicle-Us to follow him. T-

Bone sneaks up on a GUARD and knocks him out. He starts to undress him but No-Testicle-Us pushes him out of the way and with a smile and expertly strips the guard. They then knock down another guard. T-Bone and No-Testicle-Us, with a big smile, strips him also. Another one goes down and more stripping. A big guard goes, down and T-Bone finds some keys! T-Bone, Cleopatra, and No-Testicle-Us, are dressed as Guards. This of course turns Cleopatra on, and she and No-Testicle-Us can't keep their hands off of T-Bone. Heading down a hallway, the three are lost. T-Bone looks around. "This place is big as Caesar's Palace." Cleopatra corrects him,

"No, this is under the Coliseum, Caesar's Palace is much bigger."

"No, I was talking about Caesars in Vegas." Cleopatra looks quickly at T-Bone.

"Did you say Vegas or vagina?"

No-Testicle-Us is suddenly interested in the conversation, "Oh, yes, talk about vaginas and make love to both of us."

T-Bone shakes his head.

"You guys are freaks." He sees stairs heading downward. "There, stairs, that is what I have been looking for." The three of them race towards the stairs. T-Bone, Cleopatra, and No-Testicle-Us, race down the steep stairs. Finally they reach the dungeon floor. They find themselves in a huge prison underneath the Coliseum. There are prisoners in cells everywhere. T-Bone cannot find Tony, Joey, and Ralphie. Cleopatra tugs at his arm and points. In a cell, Ralphie and Joey, are in a heated argument and about to come to blows.

"Retard, retard, retard!" Ralphie goes crazy! "Jerk! Jerk! Jerk!"

Tony is just fed up, "Are you kidding me? We are in some hole with a bunch of smelly stugots and you guys are about to go off on each other?" Joey leaps at Ralphie and somehow all three end up rolling around on the floor. The guys feel a presence. They look up and see three guards standing over them. Ralphie looks at them, "*Mama mia* please, I don't want to die."

Joey takes a deep breath, "I'm too young to die."

Tony just shakes his head. "You guys are unbelievable." Tony stands up, "be men for goodness sakes. Listen, just leave these *stoliti*. Take me, just take me!" One of the Gguards reaches through the bars and grabs Tony and kisses him on lips. Shocked, Tony steps back. "What the—?"

Cleopatra, with a smile, takes her helmet off, as does T-Bone and No-Testicle-Us, both howling with laughter. T-Bone looks at the guys, "We got to go guys! Let's find the Time Machine and get the hell out of here! Trust me, its way too freaky here." T-Bone unlocks the cell door with the keys. He smiles at Maximus. "Maxi Pad let's go, you are free." Maximus shakes his head, "Leave here? Are you crazy?" He holds up a food bowl. "With all you can eat." He points out towards all the other cells. "Do you know how long it took to get this view?" Maximus shakes his head. "Give up all this to go back to my wife? Have you ever seen my wife? Kill me now. Go, go!"

Tony, Joey, Ralphie, following T-Bone, Cleopatra, and No-Testicle-Us, race out of the cell. Coming into the huge marble hallway, they look around trying to figure out where they are. Suddenly a GUARD spots them. "Halt! Who goes there?" T-Bone motions for the rest to be quiets. "It is I, T-Bone-Is-Me." Cleopatra and No-Testicle-Us giggle.

"T-Bone-Is-Me? What Battalion of Caesar's army are you with?"

T-Bone panics and doesn't know what to say. "Your mama's?"

In horror they all look at each other as the guard blows a horn and summons help. "Intruders!" Tony motions to the guys, "This way!" They all follow Tony and now with the Guards following a *'Marx Brothers'* chase ensure. Tony and everyone race down a hallway with the GUARDS snapping. With the guards right behind them they race up some stairs. They fly down another marble hallway trying to lose the them. Now there is hallway of doors, and suddenly, one opens, and it's just Cleopatra. Another door opens, and it's a guard, another door, it's Tony. Then all hell breaks loose, and everyone runs with guards chasing them. Tony and the rest race down a hall into the Main Hall. They run into more guards. Tony shoots orders as they are running, "Head back." They turn to run but it's too late. They are surrounded and there is nowhere to go.

The CAPTAIN OF THE GUARDS steps up, "Take them to Caesar."

The guards march off Tony, Joey, Ralphie, T-Bone, Cleopatra, and No-Testicle-Us.

From a balcony above, unknown to anyone, Brutus and his crew watch. "It is time."

* * * * *

BACK AT THE BARN, a hell of a lot worse for wear, Sal, Bulldog, Uncle Roscoe, and Daisy, struggle to stand up after the explosion of the Time Machine going back in time. Jimmy Two-Shoes is shaking his head.

"The coming of that machine ain't so bad but when it goes, that's an ass kicker!"

Sal, so confused and annoyed, screams, "Shut-up! We got to figure." All of a sudden, the ground starts to shake again! Sal looks at the guys,

"Get ready! They're coming back!" Sal, Bulldog, and Jimmy, have their guns ready! Daisy runs over to Uncle Roscoe.

"Don't be hanging on me I don't want no sex disease." With a loud bang and a big puff of smoke, the Time Machine appears! But instead of Tony and the guys or even Brutus, out steps Rosalina Rosa! But the gypsy babe from the psychic shop at Coney Island is no longer dressed like a gypsy. She now has on some futuristic outfit and looks unbelievably hot! Sal, Bulldog, and Jimmy Two-Shoes' jaws hit the barn floor. They have never seen such a hot woman.

Daisy has had enough. "Okay guys that's enough. She's not that hot."

Uncle Roscoe starts sniffing the air. "Hell, I'm blind, and even I can tell that is some fine woman!" Startled to see Sal and the others, Rosalina takes her futuristic remote control looking weapon and POOF! And much to the amazement of Sal and the others the Time Machine disappears right in front of their eyes. "Grab the space babe and get that weapon thing-y!!" Rosalina spins to fire off her weapon at Sal, Bulldog, and Jimmy Two-Shoes, but she is too slow. Sal blocks her hand and the weapon goes flying. She tries to jump and grab it but is no match for to the enormous amount of Italian "muscle" coming at her. She goes down in a heap with Sal, Bulldog, and Jimmy Two-Shoes, on top of her. The weapon is falling in slow motion and lands in Sal's out stretched hand.

"Yes!" A big smile comes to his lips. With Rosalina, Uncle Roscoe, and Daisy, now tied up, Sal stands in front of them. He looks at Rosalina and smiles. "So you're going to pull the "no talkie English" crap." Rosalina just looks at him. Bulldog and Jimmy Two-Shoes looks at Sal.

"You want me to plug her?"

"You plug her she'll never talk, she'll be dead."

"I never thought of that."

Sal has had enough. "That's why I do the thinking, both of you shut-up!" Sal looks at Rosalina., "Look, we don't need your machine. We're waiting here until Tony and those knuckleheads come back and we'll take theirs."

Daisy looks at Sal, "I know people and once they find out how you treated me—"

Sal once again looks at Bulldog and Jimmy Two-Shoes; "Gag her, hell with it, gag all of them!" Sal watches as Bulldog and Jimmy Two-Shoes start gagging Daisy, Uncle Roscoe, and Rosalina. "We'll be the richest guys in the world. We'll steal every treasure from the start of time." Sal holds up Rosalina's weapon. "And

Lady trust me when I say this, you will show me the true power of this "weapon" of yours." Sal smiles evilly.

* * * * *

IN A BEAUTIFUL DINING hall in true Roman fashion, guests drunk out of their minds, lie on their sides eating and drinking. Caesar is sitting at the head table and takes a bite of some food and spits it out.

"What the stugotes is going on? Take this away, it tastes like ass." Caesar burps and presses his chest as a SLAVE wipes his face. "Damn, Angina, you are bothering me, away." As the slave leaves, the doors to the Dining Hall bursts open. In comes the Guards with Tony and everyone else. "What is this?" Tony and the rest look up at Caesar, a little afraid. "My stomach is killing me and now I have to deal with this. Will I ever find peace?' The guard looks at Caesar, "Caesar, the men from the metal machine were trying to escape sir." Caesar looks once again at Tony and the rest.

"Is that you Cleopatra?"

"Yes it is Sir."

Caesar smiles, "and is that wonderful No-Testicle-Us with you?"

"As always." Caesar looks at the guards. "Free those two and feed the rest to the lions."

"But your Emperor"

"That is my command!"

Caesar rubs his belly. "Oh take them away! My stomach, get me a slave to push on my stomach!" As the guards start to usher Tony and guys out, Joey breaks free and addresses Caesar. "I know what is wrong with your stomach my Emperor." The guards grab him but Caesar puts his hand up, "Let him go." Caesar looks at Joey,

"Are you a physician?"

"No, but I love food." Joey takes a step towards Caesar.

"You're not getting enough fibre. Fibre is the god's gift to the bowels." Joey smiles, "It's like the Fed-Ex of the poop chute, trust me, what you need is a good dump."

Caesar smiles, "you know of what you speak, and where do I find this 'fibre', that you speak of?"

Joey holds up his hands, "I am going to rock your world." And with that Joey walks towards Caesar.

Inside the dining hall, Joey looks like Mario Battle on Steroids. He is chopping away while everyone in the hall is mesmerized by Joey. He's like a tornado behind the cooking table and soon he has made the world's most beautiful salad. Presenting it to Caesar, Joey smiles and Tony and the others cross their fingers. Caesar smells the salad and takes a huge bite, as everyone holds their breath. "This is quite delicious, refreshing and light, yet robust in flavour. I would add a tad more anchovies." Joey smiles, "Exactly you're Caesar-ship, that is the beauty of the culinary arts. You add a little you take away a little and then you have a great dish like this." Caesar looks at Joey, "And what do you call this wonderful dish." "There's only one thing this dish could be called, Caesar Salad."

Caesar smiles, "It does have a ring to it." Everyone applauds and cheers and begins to scoff down their salads.

"And Caesar, no disrespect but if I was you, I'd put the Vomitorium further away from the dining area."

They all look over and see people upchucking. "This man is a genius! What is your name sir?"

Joey smiles, "people just call me Joey."

Caesar smiles back, "I like it." Caesar stands, "In honour of my good friend Joey, I proclaim today, March 14th, Joey Day in all of Rome." Everyone applauds and cheers again except Tony. Tony looks at T-Bone and Ralphie.

"Did he say March 14th?"

"Yeah why?"

Tony walks up to Caesar. "Your Honour, if today is March 14th, 44 B.C., then tomorrow is the 15th of March, or better known as Ides of March." Tony gets serious fast. "Caesar it's time for a walk and talk." Caesar is confused, "A walk and talk?" Tony nods, "yeah a walk and talk. You know, like a council meeting." Caesar looks at him strangely. "We got to have a sit down, big time." Caesar motions for Tony to sit down.

March 15th on a sunny day the crowd has gathered on the Senate steps they are filled with excitement to see Caesar. They all stand as Caesar walks up the steps to the landing that leads to the Senate. His long flowing robe and Caesar's haircut are in full glory. Waiting in the crowd Brutus and his Crew are ready to attack. Brutus sees the moment is right, grits his teeth, and pulls the dagger from his robe, and starts to lunge at Caesar. Just at the last moment right before the evil dagger finds its mark, out of nowhere comes Tony. He grabs Brutus' hand and with one move takes him down hard to the floor. The crowd gasps in shock at what they just witnessed.

"You won't be killing Caesar today you scumbag, and further more, you lowlife."

Caesar turns around and it is No-Testicle-Us, with a big smile. Tony looks at Brutus, "It wasn't even Caesar you idiot." No-Testicle-Us sees the dagger on the ground.

"Honey, I like it in the back, but not with a knife."

Joey, Ralphie, T-Bone, and Cleopatra, step out of hiding, with Caesar and a bunch of his guards.

T-Bone is amazed that they actually pulled it off, "You did it man!"

Joey agrees with T-Bone, "Tony your plan worked!" Ralphie looks at Brutus and remarks one of the most famous sentences of all time, *"E tu Brutus? E tu?"*

Caesar looks at Ralphie, "I like that, can I use it?"

"It's yours, I got a million of them."

"Et tu Brutus, guards take this traitor away!" The Guards grab Brutus and his crew and haul them away. Caesar turns to Tony, "How can I ever repay you Tony?"

Joey, Ralphie, T-Bone, and Tony, all look at each other and smile. "Well there is one thing."

* * * * *

THE MAIN STREET IS jammed with people, and confetti fills the air like the ticker tape parade, and screams of delight are heard. Tony, Ralphie, Joey, and T-Bone, are all wearing togas as they stand tall and proud, as the horse drawn carriages bring them down the street. They are waving to their fans. Tony, loving the feeling, says to the guys, "I've always wanted one of these."

Ralphie agrees, "I feel like the medieval Eli Manning."

Joey just soaking it all in looks at the guys, "There must be more people here then when the Giants won the Super Bowl."

T-Bone, with Cleopatra and No-Testicle-Us, ride along, T-Bone is smiling at the ladies. "What up ladies? My album is dropping 2010 A.D. Baby!" Cleopatra smacks T-Bone as Tony looks back and yells back to the guys. The procession comes to a stop right in front of the Time Machine.

Caesar in all his glory stands next to the Time Machine and beckons Tony and the boys to join him. "You have done me a mighty service. Are you sure you don't want to stay?"

Tony feels honoured but with regret says to Caesar, "Thank you your Honour but there are many things that I have to take care in my land. I have learned from you and from my fellow Romans. It is my time to stand up and do what is right."

Tony gives Caesar a kiss on the cheek and the crowd goes crazy as Tony, Joey, Ralphie, and T-Bone, after kissing Cleopatra goodbye, climb on to the Time

Machine.   Caesar, Cleopatra, No-Testicle-Us and the crowd, wave good-bye. The earth starts to shakes. KA-BOOM! With smoke and a flash of lightening the Time Machine disappears.

*   *   *   *   *

Sal, BULLDOG, AND JIMMY Two-Shoes, start to feel the ground tremble. They pull their guns as the ground starts to shake. Sal looks at his men, "Get ready!" Huge puffs of smoke fill the air. The Time Machine appears with Tony, Joey, Ralphie, and T-Bone. In the smoke, the guys jump off the machine. With big high fives amongst each other they are unaware that Sal, Bulldog, and Jimmy Two-Shoes, are there. Tied up and gagged, Daisy, Uncle Roscoe, and Rosalina, desperately try to yell to Tony and the guys, but the guys don't even notice. Ralphie gets on his knees and kisses the ground as Tony, Joey and T-Bone still celebrate getting back to present time.

Ralphie gets up., "It's so good to be back; I'm kissing the ground." The guys laugh and then a familiar voice stops them in their tracks.

Sal has a grin on his face, "nice to have ya fellas back."

Ralphie jumps back. Tony, Joey and T-Bone know they are in a world of hurt. That's when they notice Daisy, Uncle Roscoe, and Rosalina, tied up and gagged. Bulldog ready and willing, "Nice and slow boys, hands up." Slowly, Tony and the guys lift their hands. Sal is finally glad that the right guys landed warn the boys,

"Now listen here, you boys are dead." Tony rolls his eyes and can't believe this day isn't over yet.

"There's no reason to go crazy, I'm sure we can work out a deal"

"'Work out a deal, a deal with you guys? What? Do I look like a retard to you?" Ralphie's eyes widen and his face turns red.

"That's it." Ralphie yells and does some sort of bizarre karate move and smacks Sal, Bulldog, and Jimmy Two-Shoes, in the face, *á la* a *"Three Stooges"* routine.

Sal, shocked at what Ralphie just did snaps out, "you son of a bitch! I ought to—"

Suddenly out of nowhere, just in the nick of time, a "BAA" is heard, and out of nowhere comes the sheep full bore. The sheep head butts Sal and his gun goes flying.

Tony, Joey, Ralphie, and T-Bone, see their chance, and the fight is on. Slamming into Bull Dog and Jimmy Two Shoes, their guns fly into a pile of hay. Fists are flying, and Joey takes a shot in the nose from Bulldog. Jimmy Two-Shoes takes a wicked kick to the nuts and screams in pain. Tony takes a tough left from Sal right in the nose, and then a stiff right to the eye. Meanwhile, the Sheep has races over to where Uncle Roscoe is and looks at him.

Uncle Roscoe smells the air. "Oh damn, it's the bastard raping sheep." He shakes his head, "It looks like he's going to have his way with me, again."

Daisy looks at Uncle Roscoe in horror.

Ralphie jumps on Bulldog's back and is riding him like a donkey, as he throws punches.

"Who's the 'mentally handicapped' now?!"

T-Bone and Joey fight Jimmy Two-Shoes, Sal and Tony are still going at it, and it looks like Sal is getting the best of it. With a "BAA" the sheep makes a move and starts chewing the rope quickly. The rope falls off Uncle Roscoe.

"I'm sorry I tried to kill you but I still won't kiss your balls."

Tony ducks a hard left by Sal and counters with a quick left, right, and then a left! Sal stumbles backwards. T-Bone has joined Ralphie in fighting; Bulldog and Joey and Jimmy two-Shoes are going at it, man to man. Joey hits Jimmy Two-Shoes, who goes flying into the pile of hay.

In the meantime, Uncle Roscoe has untied Daisy and Rosalina, and now the girls' race across the barn. Tony keeps the attack on Sal, knocking him into Rosalina and Daisy. Without Sal knowing, Rosalina lifts her weapon out of his pocket.

Jimmy has had just enough and grabs his gun, "okay! Freeze! Anyone moves a muscle I'm going to blast them." Jimmy Two-Shoes looks at the sheep, "And that includes the sheep!" Rosalina smiles and steps forward. Jimmy warns Rosalina, "I'm talking to you too, space lady or whatever the hell you are." Holding up the weapon, Rosalina looks at Sal, who can't believe she got the weapon.

"How the hell—"

"How I got my weapon back doesn't matter." Rosalina smiles, "what matters is what are we going to do with you creeps?"

Sal turns to Jimmy Two-Shoes, "Blast her!"

Jimmy Two-Shoes raises his gun but Rosalina beats him to the draw. Her weapon goes off! With a white flash, the tip explodes. Sal, Bulldog, and Jimmy Two-Shoes, are turned into three pigeons, they fly off through the hole in the barn. Tony, Joey, Ralphie, and T-bone, all look at each other, and then at Rosalina, who just stands there smiling.

The next day they wake up to a beautiful morning at the old barn. The birds are singing squirrels are playing as well as all the barn animals. Tony and boys load up the Sausage Truck and get ready to head back to Brooklyn. T-Bone, with a big smile, pulls up in his Escalade next to Tony and the guys.

"Hey guys if you're ever in Miami look me up! That was one hell of a trip."

Tony smiles back at T-Bone, "It sure was."

"Hey Ralphie, I want you to know I will never use the "R" word again."

"Thank you my brother."

Joey smiles at T-Bone "See ya T-Bone."

T-Bone smiles, hits the volume, and with rap music blasting, takes off down the road. As Tony and the guys watch him go, Daisy, Uncle Roscoe, and Rosalina, come up and also wave good-bye. Daisy then turns to Tony.

"You guys don't have to go back to Brooklyn you could stay here with me and Uncle Roscoe."

"No, there is no more running away. We are to man up and go back to Brooklyn and talk to Don Luciano and work things out."

Uncle Roscoe shakes his head, "You ain't my niece bitch, and since—" Uncle Roscoe grabs Daisy's ass, "you ain't that, that means we can have wild sex, all the time." Daisy faintly smiles as Uncle Roscoe leads her towards the old farmhouse. As Joey and Ralphie start to load the truck again, Tony turns to Rosalina.

"Look, I don't who you are or what you are but thank you for helping us."

"I'm not finished."

Tony smiles, "No, really thank you. It's time for me to—" Seeing Rosalina lift her weapon, fear strikes Tony. "Wait what the hell—"

It's too late, with a white flash the end of the weapon explodes and the boys are back outside of Junior's Cheesecake's and Desserts. The boys look up and see the bold writing saying lucky numbers. A clock reading two o' clock, a set of identical triplets walking by, the billboard reading 33 Exciting Flavours of Ice Tea, ten school children in matching outfits walking down the street in a row holding hands, five nuns in habits drive by in a convertible Mustang, and Tony is buying the lotto ticket at the bodega. Looking down at the lotto ticket. Everything fades to white. They are now at the one and only Time Square, lights, crowds and tons of excitement. Tony, Joey, and Ralphie, look around. Tony can't understand what just happened,

"Times Square?"

Joey looks at him, "How did we end up in Times Square?"

Ralphie shakes his head, "I can't remember a thing."

Joey is so confused, "Me either."

Tony starts to shake his head like it's all a dream, "Wow this is crazy. Where the hell have we been? What the hell has been going on?" Suddenly there is breaking news on the huge Jumbo-Tron looking over Times Square, and they hear the reporter say, "This is just in, ruins found in Rome prove that Caesar was in fact not killed by Brutus." A statue of Caesar is shown. "It seems Caesar died an old happy man of natural causes." Suddenly a picture of salad bowls appears on the screen. "And archaeologists also found the original Caesar salad bowls that he used to make his salad." The guys look at each other. Ralphie looks at the guys, "you know, this is going to sound crazy, but I think I already knew that."

Joey, agreeing with Ralphie turns to him, "You're not crazy because I think I've seen those salad bowls before."

The boys look around dazed and confused. Looking around, Tony sees a bodega. "Hey guys I'm going to get some gum." Tony heads to the bodega. As he starts to go in, some bird poop lands on his shoulder. "Oh come on!" Tony looks up and sees the three pigeons, the same three pigeons from the barn. They seem vaguely familiar to Tony but he does not remember them. He brushes the poop off and heads into the bodega. He goes into the store and grabs some gum and puts it on the counter. As he reaches for some money, a Lotto Ticket slips out of his pocket and falls to the floor. Tony bends over and picks up the Lotto Ticket and looks at the numbers. For a second, he almost tosses the ticket, but then he sees a poster behind the clerk, with Rosalina as the model that reads... JACKPOT 55 MILLION!!! Tony hands the ticket to the clerk to check the numbers. "Hey, can you check this ticket." The Clerk puts the ticket in the machine and by his reaction Tony can tell there is only one thing that could have happened. HE WON!!!

THE END

ABOUT THE AUTHORS

GIOVANNI GAMBINO & LANCE LANE

Giovanni Gambino is the author of Prince of Omerta, Undercover Secrets, and Mulberry street to Rome B.C. He was born in the province of Palermo in Sicily and grew up in Torretta, located in a mountainous area overlooking Palermo. Thirty-seven years old, he is the youngest in the family. His family moved to Bensonhurst, a neighborhood in southwestern Brooklyn, in 1985. He grew up in the underworld as the son of Don "Ciccio" Gambino. Don Ciccio was sentenced to 30 years in federal prison in 1988 and passed January, 4th 2012 in prison. Giovanni was raised and cared for by real men of honor. Out of respect for Don Ciccio these men of respect taught Giovanni about the real underworld and how to avoid precarious situations. Visit him online at giovannigambino.com

Lance Lane is a self-taught screenwriter and playwright, Lance Lane was born in Prosser Washington. The second youngest of nine children, Lance grew up in Richland, Washington and attended Hanford High School. After graduating high school, Lance moved to Los Angeles to pursue a career in acting, writing and directing.

Lance now a journeyman writer, has worked along side and with such film icons as Director John McTiernan (Die Hard), Director Tony Kaye (American History X), Playwright and Screen Writer Paul Zindel (Effect of Gamma Rays, Runaway Train), Producer Jay Julian (Kings of New York), Acting guru Lee Strasberg, Director Bobby Lewis and many more.

In recent years Lance worked on The Bleeding (Michael Madsen, Vinnie Jones) with producer Michael Tadross Jr. (Tony n' Tina's Wedding) in Wilmington North Carolina. Lance also rewrote the film Smile (Armand Assante) for Cine Tel Films also. Last year, Lance worked on an untitled Armand Assante project and with Misguided Productions' Phil and Mike Ferrara, Lance has proudly worked on Casca: The Eternal Mercenary. He is currently working on a Eric Basset (Janie Jones) production and independent film slated for shooting in the fall.

As a director Lance's films The Kings of Brooklyn (David Keith) and Junked (Thomas Jane and Jordan Ladd) have reached acclaim in the independent film circuit. Lance directed and co-wrote Kings of Brooklyn which won the New York Film and Video Festival. Junked which Lance also wrote and directed was nominated for best film in the Austin Film Festival and was nominated for a Prism Award.

Over the years Lance has worked on numerous script polishes, ghost writing assignments and treatments. Order of Redemption (Tom Berenger), Brighton Beach, Wolf Pack and Unkown Hero (Brian Kilmeade Fox News), and Baby Soldiers just to name a few.

Lance is married to actress Marion Yue, with whom he has a lovely daughter filmmaker Zoe.

He is a proud member of the Directors Guild of America, and also a member of Actor's Studio Writers and Directors Unit.